GEORGE IS TROUBLED — BY A FIELD! IT SEEMS TO BE TRYING TO TELL HIM SOMETHING. As his relationship with his partner, Barbara, falls apart, he staggers through drinks, dogs and despair trying to avoid a poltergeist and unnerving memories of his own boyhood. With dark humour and lyrical craft Ciaran O'Driscoll tells a marvellous winter's tale set in rural Italy, about the way a man deals with the relationships that he forms, and those that have formed him.

A Year's Midnight
©Ciaran O'Driscoll and Pighog Press 2012

Ciaran O'Driscoll has asserted his right to be identified as the author of this work in accordance with the Copyright, Designs and Patents Act 1998.

All rights reserved. No part of this book may be reproduced, stored in a retrieval system, or transmitted in any form, or by any means, electronic or otherwise, without the prior written permission of Pighog Press.

This novel is entirely a work of fiction. The names, characters and incidents portrayed in it are the work of the author's imagination and are not to be construed as real. Any resemblance to actual persons, living or dead, events or localities, is entirely coincidental.

Art direction and design by Aneel Kalsi
Typeset by Toby Jury Morgan
Painting by Tim Lees

ISBN 978-1-906309-25-1

First published May 2012 by
Pighog Press
PO Box 145
Brighton BN1 6YU
England UK

pp

A YEAR'S MIDNIGHT

BY

CIARAN O'DRISCOLL

PART I

George stood in the bar of the Autostrada Servizio, irritably puzzled as to why he was not being served. He was being ignored yet again. This was the story of his life. Furthermore, he didn't understand what was going on. Was there, or was there not, a queue?

Barbara understood that there was a queue, but that it wasn't an orderly queue. Or that there was an order, but it didn't take the form of a queue. She didn't subscribe to George's theory of cosmic conspiracy.

It had been a tiring day. They had named it the Day of the Hundred Tunnels, driving from Provence through Ventimiglia on the Italian border, past Genoa, and they had just veered inland towards Florence. There was farther to go, a couple of hours more to the town, and then they had to find the remote farmhouse. But they felt they should stop for a while, chiefly because of Alan, who was hungry and whingey in the back seat. Besides, it was hot – for them, that is: a beautiful afternoon in early September, a mere thirty-three degrees.

The bar was crowded. The queue that was not a queue had several tails. A large woman up at the front was arguing with an impassive bar attendant. Brandishing a lottery ticket, she turned frequently to shout at other customers in the same accusatory tone with which she addressed the mask of a face on the other side of the counter, arguing her point to everyone present, to the nation and to the world.

Purple-faced, George turned to Barbara, raising his eyes, mouthing an obscenity.

'Welcome to Italy, George,' she said.

'Welcome to bloody chaos, you mean.'

'Don't worry, it'll be quieter where we're going. Much quieter.'

Standing at the perimeter of his new home in the morning sunlight of late September, George looked into a nearby field. It was a moment of emptiness, when the visible world fills the mind without the effort of attention. In the warm sunlight, on a Sunday morning, he was drawn into the actuality of the field. A church bell rang somewhere on the borders of consciousness, and there was an occasional cry of chase and report of a hunter's rifle from the forested hills behind him. But for a long time, perhaps a minute, nothing stirred between the field and George's mind. Field, eye and mind were one and continuous. George felt an immense satisfaction in contemplating that primal containment of space.

The field ran from him to its far boundary where it was stopped in its tracks by a ploughed strip running in a transverse direction. Beyond the ploughed field, the hills sloped upwards, here and there a smallholding with rows of pointed cypresses, more ploughland, an expanse of oakwood or the regular motif of olive trees. On top of a hill, a town clustered round the bell-tower of a church.

The ragged geometry of the real: a finite green space with no compelling boundaries. Not all that green, really; not a great field agriculturally speaking; more ragged by far on the inside than its boundaries were. Uneven from bumps and hollows, unkempt from random crops of pale blue wildflowers. It was the tough abundant stalks of these flowers that gave the field its unkempt character, creating inroads, margins, stains of rust in the green space. The delicate pastel blue of the flower-heads, of course, added another dimension altogether…

By this time, George felt an old tiredness pressing from inside his chest. Pleasure was, as usual, giving way to pain. Inexplicably, he had begun to envy the field. It had some quality that he didn't possess in himself. There was a simplicity about the field, a wholeness, almost a holiness, and George saw himself as neither simple, whole nor holy. He swiped savagely at an insect that was buzzing around his head.

When he looked again, the field was still there, but different. Not much of a field really. Not worth bothering about. So what had come over him just then? He had burnt his boats and moved to this place in a last-ditch effort to wrest some tranquillity out of his life now that he had turned fifty. He badly needed a bit of Zen. And he had just allowed himself to be upset by a straggly patch of field.

'Well, you won't catch me like that again,' George said to the field. 'I've got the measure of you – nothing but grass and clay and weeds.'

'Who are you talking to, George?' a child's voice shouted behind him.

George turned his back on the field and walked towards the disused hen-shed where Alan was playing at making tea for his imaginary guests, using an assortment of stones as crockery.

'I was talking to myself,' George called as he passed the boy.

'Oh,' responded Alan. 'Would you like to have a cup of tea?'

'Not now. Siesta time.'

The hazy sun basked on the densely oak-wooded hills on the other side of the path. It basked on the terraces of young silver-green olive trees. It basked on the compound where the goats and geese had fallen quiet in the midday stillness. I have been talking to a field, thought George.

Exhausted, he climbed up the stone steps to the balcony of his first-floor apartment and went straight to the cool dark bedroom. He climbed on to the bed, lay face down and shut his eyes.

Missing him, the field whined and growled at the door of his sleep. Out of its russet fringes foxes took shape, a wild boar stepped out of its purple shades under the moon of his dream. Then the field began to seethe and heave, throwing up, one by one, a circle of standing stones. A boy appeared, naked in the centre of the field, surrounded by the megaliths.

'What's impasto?' George demanded of Barbara at supper, after a long bout of disgruntled, munching silence in which the crickets had begun, tentatively, to telephone one another, here and there a softly metallic insistent *brrr* that never gave up hope, so that the night-lines were eventually jammed with calls, half the cricket population of the countryside trying to contact the other half, who were not at home. The weather was balmy to close, and they were sitting on the first-floor balcony in a pool of light. Above their heads, moths and droning stink-bugs bounced against lamp and wall. Out of the welled-up darkness, luminous on the ear, the softly shrill din of the crickets.

'Well,' said Barbara. 'It's when you stick paint on to a canvas in large quantities, with a knife or a spatula or whatever, to make it stand out. Clots and ridges of paint, like Van Gogh's ploughed fields.'

'Oh yes of course. I keep forgetting. Laying it on with a trowel, so to speak?'

'It's always struck me as being a bit over the top. A bit too expressive, and usually of troubled emotions.'

'And we wouldn't want that kind of thing now, would we?'

'If you're working yourself up – yet again – to one of your diatribes about the prissiness of my watercolours –'

George raised a hand in a gesture of truce. 'Sorry. I just thought – '

'We came here for serenity, George. Do I have to remind you again? For you, that meant giving up writing for a year, because you thought it had caused your breakdown. But I'm just an amateur watercolourist. I enjoy my painting, prissy as it may be. And I have no intention of painting a distressed masterpiece that will drive me to suicide.'

'And fair play to you, Missus.' George took an impatient gulp of wine, rose, went and leaned his elbows on the balcony ledge, looked up at the sky milky with stars, returned to his chair, filled his wine-glass again. The cricket sound poured

into the awkward silence. Barbara yawned, took a clasp out of her hair. Time for bed.
'Do you know what?' George said eventually. 'I envy you. You are what you are, you do what you do, and there's nothing more.'
'I've worked at that,' Barbara rejoined sharply. 'I don't want anything more. And I thought you came here to work on not wanting anything more?'
George felt it was time for Barbara's massage. She would like that. He went behind her chair and began to knead her bare shoulders. She sighed contentedly.
'Mmm. That's nice. Up a bit. There.'
George spoke softly into her ear.
'You know, my grandmother told me a story once about coming home from a dance when she was a young woman and deciding to take a short cut across the fields to her cottage. There was one field she couldn't get out of; she was there all night. She walked and walked, around in circles, stung by nettles, torn by thistles and brambles. It was only with the first light that she was released from her terror. When she got home, her mother told her that she had gone into a fairy field. And that it was a punishment for sneaking out to the dance.'
'Mmm. Down a bit. Yes, there. What's the point, George? Or is this just a bedtime story?'
'Well, there is a point, but I'll tell you some other time.'
'You can tell me now, as long as you keep massaging.'
'OK, so. It's all to do with how I keep remembering things from my childhood since I came here. It's like being transported back in time. For example, we've been sitting here for hours and not a single car has passed up or down the road. I can imagine us in six months' time sitting here the way my grandmother used to sit at her kitchen window, saying things like "There she's gone up the road. I wonder where she's going?" And hours later, "Here's she's back, with a brown paper parcel." '

13

Barbara laughed. 'And what of it? We could do with a bit of rural idiocy. But we're not going to allow too much of that to happen, are we? We're learning Italian so we can get by and meet the people. And don't forget exercise, George. You've got a pot belly, and there are so many hill walks around here. The hours and hours you used to spend at your writing desk you can now spend climbing the hills. You're very restless, you can walk your restlessness off. I remember when I was in that Peak District walking club, how happy and content my body was to sit down and take a meal at the end of the day. Up a bit...there.'

George grimaced at Barbara's reminder of their Programme of Action,which he had facetiously nicknamed the Anglo-Irish Agreement. There was something more pressing he needed to tell her – how he too, like his grandmother, was becoming trapped in a field. There was a fairy field right beside them here in Italy, and his mind couldn't get out of it. But as if his steady massaging of Barbara's soft, suntanned back was dispelling the fog his thoughts had entered, he quickly brightened up. His hands began to rove further and engage in a different kind of touch, while Barbara's sighing quickened. Finally, he brought his hands around to her breasts, teased the nipples erect between his fingers.

The landlord's dogs erupted in a fit of barking. A car was approaching up the dusty road. Roar of an engine, beam of headlights swallowed by the night.

'There goes someone with a brown paper parcel,' Barbara giggled.

George led Barbara to the bedroom. The dogs settled down again on their beds under the balcony, the crickets trilled on undiminished, a giant black egg-shape peered from the golden egg-cup of the dark.

That night, George lay awake for a long time, all kinds of conflicting ideas going through his discontented head, while the watercolourist slept peacefully beside him. He worried through his various intermingled insecurities, until an incongruous image flashed on the screen of his torments. It was one of the landlord's dogs, a female Alsatian, smoking a roll-up. Lips closed on the flimsy tissue paper, she pulled on it deeply but carefully, trying to get the maximum draw without tearing the cigarette. The image was enough to make George laugh out loud in the dark room, and to relax him. He fell asleep instantly.

Next morning, however, as he lay dozing in bed, he half-dreamt, half-imagined the Alsatian skulking among the wild chicory flowers in the field, having a surreptitious drag. She was discovered there in the early light by a television crew, and prevailed upon to give a reluctant interview. How long had she been smoking, and why did she begin? She had been smoking, she said, ever since her hysterectomy. She had always wanted to smoke, but thought that as long as she was able to have puppies, it wouldn't have been fair on them. But after her operation, she had felt free to indulge herself.

And why had she always wanted to smoke? The viewers of breakfast television were treated to the spectacle of the big mournful brown eyes close up, as she hesitated about her answer, and the producer back in the studio began to worry about impatient channel zappers. Well, she said at last, I had observed that my former master smoked, particularly when he was under stress. It seemed to have a calming effect. I have always suffered terribly from my nerves, you know... Another close-up: two big tears formed in the two big doggy eyes.

The interviewer's attention was diverted by the crackle of the producer's voice on his headphones: *Be sure and ask for the canine position on abortion. And don't let the mutt go on for too long.*

The Alsatian continued. I suppose, she said, it will come as a surprise to many of your viewers that a dog, especially an Alsatian, should suffer as terribly as I do from nerves. But we are actually more sensitive than you are. We mourn not only the loss of our own kind but the loss of our human friends as well, especially the children. My nerves are shot entirely from loss and mourning, especially since my former master never excluded me from the house, and allowed me to curl up on the floor beside him every night when he was watching television. And it was from watching the news on television that my troubles began. Night after night, I watched the suffering of humans and their children in war-torn and famine-stricken countries...

Close the interview! came the voice of the anxious producer over the headphones.

What is your position on abortion? the interviewer asked. A change came over the Alsatian. She perked up enormously, picked up her tobacco pouch and Rizzla papers and rolled a nonchalant cigarette. I'm glad you asked me that, she said, but if you think you're going to get a halfways decent answer in the short time you're allowing me, you're barking up the wrong tree. Oh my God, *Barking!* she hooted.

At last she stopped laughing and, taking a long drag on her cigarette, wound up her interview: I'd like to take this opportunity to say hello to my new friend George from Ireland, without whose dire dilemma I wouldn't be here in this field this morning, and wouldn't have had the opportunity of not airing my views on abortion. Watch this space, George; watch this space.

With this, the Alsatian did a disappearing act, taking television crew and countryside with her. A loud bang of words exploded in George's ears, thunderous as the voice of the Almighty: WATCH THIS FIELD!

Wildly agitated, George jumped out of bed and ran down, still in his pyjamas, to the bluff overlooking the field. But there was nothing below only the field itself – to not air his views on, to not write about, only to watch.

The landlord had assumed that George, being a writer, would want to write, and had thoughtfully placed a desk at the bottom of the smaller of the two bedrooms in the apartment. This bedroom was given to Alan, but seeing that he was going to school, George had the use of it five days a week from nine to four, and from nine to twelve on Saturdays: such was the length of the Italian school week.

Even though he was not writing, initially George spent as much time in Alan's room as if he had been on a six-month deadline for *War and Peace*. It was a kind of Zen exercise: the time he used to spend writing, revising and editing, was now spent in 'centering', meditation, and for the most part in a state of pleasant mooning blankness, recharging the batteries that had been depleted during his breakdown.

On the morning of the smoking Alsatian, however, he went straight to Alan's room as soon as he had regained some composure, and began looking out the small window beside his desk, abandoning his Zen-like exercises in favour of an alert scrutiny of the field and whatever revelations it might have in store.

For a period, he spent so much time watching the field that he could have observed the progress of the wild chicory's transitory flowers, blooming and withering in the course of a single day. But he didn't notice that; it was Barbara who had told him about it. He was watching for something more sombre and significant. The field remained bland, however: the teeth of the grass smiled back inanely at him; the shadows of clouds came and went.

Gradually, it began to dawn on him that a certain latitude

had to be permitted in the interpretation of the mission he had been given. He didn't have to lie awake at night, for instance, because the field, if it wanted him, would appear in his dreams. Surely, therefore, he didn't have to stay at the bloody window all day. Would he miss something if he took a walk? Absolutely not. The field would see to it that he was informed of an imminent event.

On the other hand, he puzzled about the precise amount of leeway he was allowed. Might he go on trips to other parts of Italy? Would the projected Christmas visit to his mother in Ireland be tolerated? It became obvious to George that whatever power emanated from the field had to be concentrated locally; that its range of influence, like that of a lot of electromagnetic and psychic phenomena, could be only a few miles. It was always the same with such fissures opening up in the ordinary world: people went on pilgrimages to Lourdes, for instance; they didn't stay at home and wait for the miracle to reach them in their living room or garden. Or they didn't go halfway to Medjugorje and hope for the best. On the other hand, they wouldn't need to be right up beside the Virgin to feel the power, as long as they were in the locality.

He concluded that he was expected to stay in the neighbourhood, but not expected to interrupt the normal routines of life, like sleeping, eating, shopping in the town, taking Alan to school, going on walks and so on. His duty was like that of a caretaker, keeping a general eye on the field.

By Christ, but it's good to be alive, thought George. It's good to see the landlady's ample body over there, bending to tend the herbs.

She was bending like a figure in a Vermeer; time had been stopped by the still air and the soft light. He felt that it was forever, this scene arrested in perception. The entrance had been stumbled upon again, and the space had suddenly become infinite. This was not a time to tease thoughts out of the sensuous – he had made that mistake too often before; not now as the lantern-leaves of this oak tree redistributed their soft intensities of radiance, and the field framed by the light-infused foliage unfurled its narrative of hazy sun and shadow. To be now is to be infinite under the sky. To be now is becoming, crossing the infinite space between nothingness and fullness. The landlady has gone, taking with her her ample backside, but it has left, as it were, an imprint of promise on the afternoon. It has been there, and therefore it will be there.

George raised his arms like a weightlifter, inhaling deeply. He danced a little jig and then, a shot-putter, stood crouched on one leg, coiled and ready to spring, his right hand holding the shot against his neck. His arm drove out and up, the weight behind it of his whole body lurching forward to land on the other previously suspended foot. The metal ball floated through the air on a graceful arc which brought it thumping into the sodden ground several inches beyond the little flag that marked the previous best throw, on a raw late afternoon in spring, at the Munster Colleges Sports in Cork. His fellow boarders roared wildly, classmates and fellow athletes of his college poured over and under the rope at the boundary of the competitive area, knocking over a sign that read *Danger Field Events in Progress*, to hug him, to shake his hand fervently. Even that stern monk, the sad-faced dean of discipline, disregarded propriety and came up to say *Congratulations. You've done the college proud.*

The sense of achievement, of gratified exhaustion, his body happy with giving its utmost and deserving a few days' rest and indulgence, was augmented by the relief he felt because he knew the dean must now look leniently on the discovery of a detective novel with a naked woman on the cover in his bedside locker during one of the routine raids conducted by the head prefects. Brother Joseph might even bake a lemon cake, his favourite dessert, to celebrate his medal, his victory. All this on account of what he had done for the morale and the future intake of the college; the notices appearing in the *Cork Examiner* and the *Evening Echo* would be an advertisement for its sporting ethos.

All this, his world of striving and coming into his own, ought surely to have been the essence of the memory, but he found it had been reduced to mere detail. Over the years, the background had taken over, as landscape had usurped the space for the saints in Renaissance paintings: the rawness of the late spring afternoon under a cloud-driving sky, the trees and buildings, a figure in an overcoat exiting through a distant turnstile, the faraway barking of a dog. Whenever he thought of his days in that boarding school, what he remembered mostly was the raw quality of afternoons in February or March, the path that led uphill through the monastery pastures to the sports field, standing on the edge of that field, pausing briefly in his retrieval of a discus to glance down at Cork Harbour, maybe to watch a ship on its way out, hearing a ghostly hoot of departure carried up from the sea roads as he followed the flight track of a javelin.

Elsewhere. That's where he had lived his life up to now. Reality had always been down the road, across the sea, a few days or a few years into the future. But soon it would be here and now, no longer somewhere else. All he had to do was keep a close watch out for a momentous field event, down there, at the bottom of the bluff. Then he would learn the secret of being centered in himself, in the present. No longer a figure in an overcoat exiting through a turnstile at the periphery of the action, he would become the centre from which the action sprung. No more would he think that what's elsewhere was him and what's here and now was something else. On went the flow of thought, and all the time George was standing like a statue of an athlete who has just putted the shot.

And that rotten bastard, the dean of discipline, who decided after all that he couldn't make fish of one and flesh of another, and gave me eighteen whacks of the sawn-off billiard cue, nine on each hand, all for a detective novel with a naked woman on the cover, one that had no descriptions of sex worth talking about, nothing only *She gave herself to him totally*, and *She could feel his sex hard inside her*. I was so confused I spent days pondering that, not sure if his sex was his prick or something else, and wondering where he put it to get it inside her, if it was his prick; was it up her arse he put it, and how soon after that would a baby pop out. And what did *totally* mean? Was it that she let him feel everything, because the girls I eventually went out with used to have forbidden zones? But that's all gone now, thank God, and I'm free. Free!

George skipped free of his statuesque position, did a cumbersome twirl, punched the air two or three times like a boxer, clapped his hands and rubbed them together vigorously. He sauntered down the slope and walked though the field, knowing in his heart that new developments beckoned. There was a long strip of ploughland in front of him that stopped his field in its tracks: deep brown earth, freshly opened, a flock of pigeons rising from it as he approached through the tangled scrag of chicory flowers.

When he went to London and met Barbara, her permissiveness had been a revelation. What his Irish girlfriends had considered depraved, such as oral sex, intercourse from behind, watching it in mirrors, Barbara had either taught him herself or considered quite normal. Even anal intercourse was not ruled out: she had said that she considered it quite naughty, but with a kind of complicitous tone that seemed to suggest *Why don't you try me on that one?*

The light was fading as George returned along the damp dirt track. In the woods beside him, the wild boars bided their time; after nightfall they would cross the road. A farmer living farther up the hill would see one in his car's headlights, and stop just in time to admire the compact agglomeration of savage muscle, regretting that he hadn't his gun. The boars would dig frantically in the field, rending the grass, wounding the surface as they burrowed muddy holes in their search for roots.

One Monday morning Barbara sat on a low wall at the top of a flight of steps in the centre of the town. At her back was a bar with a terrace overlooking the narrow main street. The bar was closed, but two old men were sitting at a table on the terrace, smoking and reading papers in the October sunlight. Just below her was a statue of Garibaldi, around which a flight of steps parted like a stream around a rock, coming together again and sweeping down to join the river of the street. Across the piazza from her corner was a government office which George had entered some time ago. Apparently, though he hadn't imparted much information about it, he was looking for a *permesso di sioggiorno* – a residency permit.

Barbara was thin and sensuously well preserved. Her black hair (with a few scarcely noticeable strands of grey) was cut to a medium length. Sunglasses covered her blue eyes. She had a slender nose and surprisingly full lips. She liked to dress below her age, but here in Italy she felt safer staying conservatively smart, and today she was wearing a cotton print dress, a pink cardigan and flat shoes.

The piazza on whose perimeter she sat was not beautiful by Italian standards, but Barbara was admiring the houses around her, all of which had balconies with ornately wrought railings, adorned with pots of geraniums and basil. There were more pots of geraniums hanging here and there, as if self-suspended, in the many-toned facades of mortared brick and stone, and occasional ceramic bas-reliefs of the Virgin and saints glinted their bright colours from nooks in the walls. Some of the balconies were still covered with summer awnings, which flapped suddenly whenever a flock of pigeons alighted or took off.

The building which George had entered to engage in bureaucratic rites of passage was a big austere block of a thing, but like all the other houses on the square, it had elegantly arched windows, disposed in an asymmetrical way. With their play of law and disorder, they mocked Barbara's expectations of stolid regularity. Big windows were paired with small ones, there was no window at all where one was needed to complete a 'proper' row, a small one was inserted at the end of a row of bigger ones, and so on. She shuddered suddenly, felt a twinge of homesickness.

The sun poured its diminished heat into the piazza. So soft and mild for a day in late autumn, but there were innumerable signs of approaching winter, not just the yellowing of leaves in potted plants, but the immobility, the not-much-happening. Men and women emerged out of the piazza's corners, one by one, with good intervals of time between them. They passed Barbara, with or without a *buon' giorno* (some were preoccupied, lost in thought), and went up or down the steps about their business, some to the doctor's, others to the hairdresser's. The piazza, the highest level of the hill town, was life's stage, and people made their brief appearances there, and left.

Monday morning was *always* quiet, of course, but even last Thursday morning when the market was in full swing, to Barbara the whole place had been a chattering of swallows under an autumn sky. She had been impressed by the immensity of the sky under which the market happened and noticed how the light was no longer the light of summer. The air was clearer, she saw the moving figures clearly in this motionless light, the gesticulating arms of bargainers (which seemed to have slowed in her memory), the greeting and embracing. Several streets were lined with stalls, and the stalls were offering cheeses and clothes, hams and antiques, anything at all from roast suckling pig to second-hand audio cassettes. And she remembered her shock on seeing, among all these goods, tiny birds for sale as food, strung up like necklaces of onions. She had heard about these morsels of gourmet delectation before, but to see them hanging in the brute reality of a market stall was far more unsettling than to be told about them.

Barbara sighed with a new sense of satisfaction. Her memory of the market was so clear, and she could sense a creative stir within her, a primal painterly urge to rework and transmute the scene – and to include somehow in her picture the sense of shock she felt at seeing the small strung-up songsters for the first time.

She suddenly felt that her visual imagination would come into its own here in Italy, away from the confining routines of work and home, in stretches of time available to sit like this, randomly observing, and let her thoughts off the leash. The very *idea* of attempting to realize the kind of picture that had just occurred to her would have been beneath her conservative dignity up to now. It was liberating to feel that she was beginning to let go of her timidity, that she was capable of more. When she applied for the year's leave of absence from teaching, she offered 'to develop my painting' as the reason, more as a ploy to make it harder for the school to refuse than out of any conviction. But now she was prepared to credit that something in her had pushed for the affirmation of that motive in the face of her reluctance to lie to the school board. She sat there happily on the low wall in the piazza and really didn't care if George never came out of the bureaucratic building. Her only regret was that she had not brought her sketch pad with her, to make a start on a work which she might ironically call *Songbirds Under an Autumn Sky*.

But the mere flicker of a George-thought was enough to blemish her content. George was in the building, and he would eventually come out. And the only reason she was sitting on the low wall, letting her thoughts pleasantly wander, was that she was *waiting for George*. And George was on the verge of becoming a problem. He was threatening to be more of an impediment to her year of freedom than an adjunct. This was particularly the case in relation to one of the founding principles of the grand design: the hope, amounting to an assumption, that the year would lead to a renewal of their sex life. What rubbish that had turned out to be.

Now Barbara found herself drawn in to remembering the beginnings of her relationship with George, when they made love every day. She had liked his bestial weight on top of her, his grunting bed-creaking unstoppable drive to enter her. George had kindled in her a perception of her body's allure, an erotic narcissism that her husband had never managed to arouse. And in return she had liked teasing him with tight clinging jeans, knowing that as far as George was concerned, her crowning glory was her bottom. As he had frequently put it, she had a bottom 'to beat the band'. His crudely expressed sexual candour, rather than dampening her desire, had inflamed her. But she didn't want to wear those kinds of jeans in Italy, because of what she had been told about the forwardness of Italian men. It seemed that Italian husbands forgot their marital status about a thousand times a day.

She had one special pair of jeans with vertical stripes which used to drive George mad: it was the way the stripes oscillated when they got to her bottom, as if approaching it sent a straight line into a loop; the way all the lines did it simultaneously, unanimously, by spontaneous acclaim, half of them looping off in one direction around one buttock and the other half in the other direction around the other. George had told her that if he looked at these stripes long enough, he began to see after-images of striped Barbara-bottoms, and nothing could calm him down except voracious grope and grasp, leading to swift and thunderous consummation.

That was what had flattered Barbara about George's rude and constant attentions in the early days of their relationship. But things had changed. His libido had gone into an 'on-off' mode: a few weeks hot, a few weeks cold. Then, a bit like the cows in Joseph's dream, the cold weeks devoured the hot weeks, and there was nothing but cold.

Barbara shivered. She shifted her position on the low wall, crossed one of the many borders between shadow and light that dappled the morning.

George had been hot for a few weeks after their arrival in Italy, and now he had gone cold again. But there was something else that troubled her: a discovery. One afternoon she had come into their bedroom and found him gazing at his naked self in the wardrobe mirror. He was posing like a model, sideways to the mirror, chest out, pot belly tucked in, arms akimbo, the thumb and forefinger of each hand resting on his hips. He had made a joke of it, of course, but Barbara had immediately suspected that he might be gay, or at least bisexual. In fact, bisexuality might better explain his on-off attentions, his going through successive periods of heterosexual and homosexual energy. On the other hand, the fact that the lean cows of his frigidity had swallowed the fat cows of his lust over the three years before their arrival in Italy might suggest that he was really deep down seriously gay, not just bisexual; and that his sexual zeal during the first few weeks of their year away should be regarded as a mere blip brought on by the unaccustomed heat of September and their being thrown together without any other friends.

Hearing his familiar griping voice, she looked up and saw George making his way across the piazza in his lime green T-shirt, khaki shorts and friar's sandals. Head down, he was talking to himself. Or rather, cursing to himself: she could discern venomous fucks and shits, which stood out in his garbled mutterings. At last he looked up and noticed her. He came over and stood beside her, sulkily waiting for an expression of interest in his doings.

Barbara looked at George appraisingly. She had a penchant for looking at him as a stranger in whom she might or might not be interested. Except for the pot belly, he was still a fine specimen: somehow his frame had refused to add fat anywhere except in the middle. She imagined that if he kept on guzzling food and drink at his accustomed rate, his belly would burst under the pressure of this ban by his other parts on the offloading of fat from the centre. Then he would be laid out, his belly carefully stitched up, as a fairly tall, handsome corpse, with a short grey beard and a bald patch in the centre of his head like a monk's tonsure. The dreamy blue eyes would be closed by two coins, the perfectly placed medium-sized ears attending to silence, the thin lips motionless, the largish nose with its wide nostrils no longer breathing. Gay men would travel from all over the world to mourn his beautiful corpse, to take a last look at this David they had lost the chance of enjoying. Speechless, they would admire the lucent skin, the Marilyn Monroe legs, the magnificent bouncy bottom, the curvy shoulders...

'Well?' Barbara asked, as George seated himself beside her. 'What was all that about?'

'It's a bloody disgrace,' he blurted. 'Anyone would think we weren't from the EU but from Ulanbataar or somewhere equally godforsaken. Do you know that it's going to take ages to get a residency permit – ages?'

'But what's the hurry? Hasn't the landlord told you that you can stay as a tourist for three months at a time? And we're going to Ireland for Christmas. All we have to do is sign on again when we come back – for another three months.'

'But that's the trouble. I'm not going home for Christmas. I can't.'

'You *can't*? Why not?'

'Look, can we go and have a cappuccino somewhere?' George got up and looked around. 'Ah. There's a bar right behind you. Let's go.'

'It's closed this morning. It won't be open till twelve.'

George looked at his watch. 'That's in ten minutes. I need a coffee. We'll sit over there and wait.'

The two old men stared at them briefly as they sat at the only other table on the terrace.

'Well then,' said Barbara, dangerously quiet-spoken. 'What's all this about not going home for Christmas?'

'I am definitely not going home to my mother for Christmas. You can go and bring Alan with you. But I'm staying here.'

'Sod you, George!' Barbara exploded, so that the two old men looked up suddenly, discommoded in their sunny tranquillity. 'We discussed all this, agreed on it, and arranged it. And now you're opting out, and what really annoys me is that you are so unforthcoming about it. Would you mind telling me why? Or is it all too dark and beyond the ken of a lesser being?'

'Keep your inferiority complex out of this,' George snapped. 'I've just come to the very sensible conclusion that it's a waste of time to go to Ireland for Christmas. Why go home to Mother at all, mine or yours, when we're staying abroad only for a year? I mean, it's not as if we're life exiles like the usual crowd who go home for Christmas.'

'Bullshit,' Barbara hissed. 'We discussed that very point, remember? You said it would be nice for me to meet your mother. And you also said – and here the hypocrisy and condescension of it makes me cringe – you also said that the wild western coast might be a good subject for my paintings. That it would help me to move on. As if I couldn't move on here in Italy. The only reason I agreed to go to Ireland was because I thought you wanted to. Then I began to look forward to it, muggins that I am. You are such a retentive bastard, George.'

George banged the table with his fist, startling one of the old men into dropping his cigarette. The other clicked his teeth in disgust, and they both stared censoriously at the couple for a long time, muttering *sotto voce*. Remembering that he was applying for a residency permit, George tried to conciliate the old men. '*Scusate*,' he said. '*Le donne*', and spread his arms in a broad gesture implying *What can we do with the women?* The veterans were somewhat placated, and deigned to remain in their seats.

'You prick,' said Barbara.

George covered his face with his hands and stayed silent for a long time. When he spoke again his tone had changed from annoyance and sarcasm to an awed hush. 'Actually, it's a serious business. A very serious business. And ironically you are right in what you just said: it is dark – darker than I ever bargained for. I can't even explain it to myself. Maybe I'm going mad, but I have to see it through.'

'What are you trying to say?'

'I am going to learn something. I am going to be told something. I am going to discover something,' George continued in his hushed tone. 'But I have to stay here or it won't happen. That's the long and the short of it. Call it an intuition, a beam into my head from outer space, insanity, or whatever name you want to put on it. I don't know what it is, except that it's a certainty, a categorical imperative. And I couldn't even leave if I tried.'

'I can't believe this is happening,' Barbara moaned, and it was her turn to cover her face. But, apart from being upset and angry, she was also feeling responsible for the part she might have played in what she saw as George's relapse: his writing had brought him to one nervous breakdown, and now his not writing was causing another; the rural simplicity of *not wanting any more* had got to him into a worse way than writing ever could.

A young man noisily unlocked the door of the bar and came to take their order. When his coffee came, George made heavy weather of opening the sugar sachet, and worked his spoon in his cup as if the act of stirring needed enormous concentration. Barbara ignored her coffee, numbed, listening in the balmy sunshine to a voice from another world.

'You see, the truth is I don't have to go to Ireland. My childhood is here. It is all around me. The brown paper parcels. The voices of children at school, reciting sing-song rote. The rabbit-hunting. My grandmother's fairy field is here, too, right beside the house. And that is where it will all be revealed. I *know* it will.'

The house where Barbara and George were staying was bounded on three sides by forested hills and on the fourth by a flat valley which was itself almost entirely hill-surrounded. The valley was the bottom of a saucer, and the rim of the saucer had bits chipped off on either side, and through these openings a dual carriageway poured its traffic to and from the city, bypassing the town, which climbed the slope between the fissures and was crowned with a ruined castello draped in scaffolding.

The house rested on a low shoulder, in a clearing, difficult to see from the dusty potholed byroad which reached it from just outside the town. It was an old farm dwelling with thick stone walls and a terracotta-tiled roof, surrounded by herbs in pots, in neat hedges, in trimmed clumps: rosemary, oregano, thyme, lemon balm, sage. There were a few small lemon trees, a potted chilli plant, various exotic flowers, and, strewn everywhere with a kind of planned negligence, objects such as a bed end, a tilted handcart, giant wine bottles in wickerwork coverings, an Aladdin's lamp dangling from a privet tree, assorted tiles in homogeneous heaps, two squat wooden barrels, and a curious arrangement whereby the branching end of a tree trunk was turned upside down to serve as a table stand for a very wide shallow terracotta bowl which overflowed with creeping thyme.

The present owner had converted the house into four apartments, two on the ground floor (where animals were traditionally kept), and two on top, which had outside stairs and balconies. George and Barbara had rented an upstairs one, its balcony looking out over an enclosure where goats and geese coexisted, and rising woodland.

In the apartment below George's lived the landlord and his wife. The landlord was Irish, a Northerner whom George had initially contacted through a mutual friend in Dublin. He had been in Italy for thirty years, and lectured on English language and literature at a city university. His wife was a German woman who taught her own language, literature and culture in one of the city's language schools.

For most of the year, the other two apartments were only very occasionally occupied, usually at weekends, by Romans or other big-city dwellers wanting a break in the country. In summer they were more constantly booked, but not always, since the landlord's agritourism venture was in its infancy. Originally he had supplemented his lecturing income by self-sufficiency, growing olives and keeping geese, Tibetan goats and hens. He liked to be surrounded by animals, perhaps owing to a nostalgia for the farm of his Irish childhood. He had three dogs: Babs, a female Alsatian; Giorgio, a mongrel with a dominant percentage of Border Collie; and a small bushy-tailed Fox Terrier bitch named Carinosa. The landlord's animals were an added promotional feature when he turned to agritourism. So too was his garden produce, which he would personally deliver to his guests with great ceremony, according to availability: tomatoes, courgettes, aubergines, broccoli and potatoes. He was also glad to present his clients with an occasional egg or two, but his hens weren't great layers.

On the edge of the shoulder on which the house stood, the hens' sheds were concrete compartments which were originally intended for pigs. The hen population occupied two out of four of these, and a large freezer had been installed in the third, a grim reminder of their last end if the hens had been capable of recognizing its function. The hens were free to range around the place; they were free-range, thoroughly organic creatures.

The fourth shed was perpetually locked. George had noticed this. He had asked Alan, whom the landlord was beginning to take with him on his farmyard tours, to try and find out what was in it. But the landlord had warned Alan to stay away from it. He told him there were 'not nice things' in there.

A narrow path like a goat track ran between the sheds and the short steep drop to the level ground. George could often be found standing on this track, looking down over the drop at his field. It was a good view, though he had to crane his neck to peer between the cypresses. *A single field which I have looked upon*: out of its many aspects, in the changing light of one day or its stealthy seasonal changes, might come the annunciation he was expecting – a blocked memory, perhaps, or an apocalyptic warning.

One night after supper the landlord, Rogero – he had adopted the Italian version of his name – and his wife, Mathilde, were sitting on either side of the huge open fireplace in their downstairs apartment. They rarely had time to talk to one another about personal matters because of the demands of their teaching posts, various extra-curricular and social activities, and the administration of the agritourism venture; but mainly from lack of inclination. They usually ate separately, in city restaurants or pizzerias, before returning home, and spent the evenings preparing lectures, filling in endless forms for the voracious Italian bureaucracy, and attending to the plants and animals.

It was Mathilde who had asked for time to discuss something urgent, and Rogero had gathered logs from the pile beside the sheds, lit a fire and opened a bottle of wine, in a show of readiness. It was what he would have done to welcome an off-season guest.

'It's that man,' said Mathilde at last, in a voice portentously hushed, when she had settled into the comfort of the log fire and the wine. 'That George. What are we going to do about him?'

'What do you mean? Has he done something?' The landlord sat up in surprise.

'No. Not yet.'

'Not yet? What on earth does that mean?'

'Well, he's odd. Surely you've noticed? He's always skulking about the place. I keep finding him in the most unlikely places, in the strangest postures, when I'm tending the herbs. And he never says a word. He simply scowls and darts off. Then I find him somewhere else, peering though a window, staring at something or other.'

A cloud of smoke drifted out over Rogero, making him cough. He busily adjusted the chimney damper, then settled back in his chair before answering.

'He's a writer isn't he? Writers can be odd. And they often poke around looking for sources of inspiration, which makes them seem even odder.'

'As long as he doesn't poke around too far. And I'm sure you remember what that means.'

'Oh that,' said Rogero with distaste. 'You know as well as I do that it would take a small bomb to open that. And as for peering in the window, you sealed it up personally.'

'All well and good, but – '

'But what? We're talking here about a respected writer. He's *fairly* well known. Or so Francis told me. He's had a novel published, and Francis saw a favourable review somewhere or other.'

'A pity Francis didn't tell you he's such a boor. He exudes hostility, Roger. Still, if that's all it was, I think I could put up with him. Though I hardly think his paltry amount of fame compensates for bad manners. But it's more than that. I feel there's more, much more. He frightens me. There's something demonic about him. I'm afraid he's going to do something terrible before he leaves.'

'But you're an expert on German Literature, my dear. *You* ought to know more about the Faustus theme than I do. I mean, there's *supposed* to be a demonic side to creativity, isn't there? Writers are often totally egotistic, self-absorbed, half-mad, because of this mental wrestling with their demon...'

'That's fine, as long as we don't have to put up with it. Awful people can produce great books. I'll read the books. But we have made a life for ourselves here, after much difficulty, and I won't have that man ruining it. He's a bad man, Roger. I know it. There's something destructive there. Something is driving him, and it's not creativity.'

'I haven't noticed,' Rogero said limply. It was an all-too-familiar motif, this paranoia, and he found it harder and harder to muster any sympathetic reassurance. 'Anyway,' he continued defensively, 'what are we supposed to do? Evict him? He pays rent – or at least his woman friend does. And we need the money.' The idea of money rallied Rogero to a spirited defence of taking no action. 'Guests who stay a whole year are worth dozens of weekend comers and goers. And if he skulks about the place, so much the better. We're out most of the time, and the dogs are useless, as you know from the burglary two years ago. Maybe it's good that we have an oddity with a demonic rictus darting in and out of the shrubbery.'

'That's as may be, as long as he doesn't attack me. And that's what I'm afraid of. There's a kind of violence about him, and it's sexual, an unsavoury sexual undercurrent. I'm afraid of him, Roger.'

A spume of sap oozing from one of the logs spat and hissed in the flames. Twigs blackened, snapped off and were devoured, glowing incandescent, becoming white ash, shrinking, collapsing into nothing. Rogero stared gloomily at the grotesque creatures forming and disappearing in the embers. He knew too well what had happened between them. And now she saw base sexual designs everywhere, and nowhere sex that wasn't base. Where was their first love, all that giving to one another, the happiness that asked no questions? The flames had devoured everything. What was the use? He spoke slowly, with suppressed anger.

'The man is a writer. OK, he's odd. He's paying good rent. We have lots of overheads. He hasn't laid a finger on you, and unless and until you have something more to go on than fear and suspicion, he stays.'

'I knew you'd say that.' Mathilde rose with dignity, leaving her half-finished glass of wine on the hearth. 'It's all just a woman's hysterical imagination. Well, don't say I didn't warn you. I have an early lecture tomorrow. Goodnight, Roger.'

'What can I say? I'll keep a closer eye on him from now on, and we'll discuss it again.'

'That's the very least you can do.' Mathilde went to her bedroom.

Rogero stayed up for a long time, finishing the bottle of wine, staring into the purgatory of the fire. He knew it was all to do with their not having a child. He had never wanted one, of course. Now he wasn't so sure. He liked bringing Alan with him in the morning to feed the animals. There was something paternal about it; he wanted to explain things about the farm to him and tell him stories, he couldn't deny the feeling the boy had aroused in him, an innocence he thought was gone, a guiding instinct. It was many things, hard to express. But Mathilde had looked at the Gorgon and been turned to stone.

They never discussed it now. You spend your life trying to make something of yourself in a foreign country, starting from nowhere, and become a respected professor. You amass property, fields and woods, and become something more; you tackle an obstinate language rather than hide in an English-speaking enclave complaining about the natives, and in the end they accept you, they come to you for advice, they even put you on the town council. You spend your days doing one thing, and life turns out to be another. There must be another life to go beyond this, into the future…

'Alan! School!' George roared from the balcony. 'Alan, I won't call you again!'

'Coming.' Alan ran up to where the red Toyota was parked beside the balcony steps. Red-faced, George was waiting for him by the car. Big fatty.

'Where's your schoolbag? Go up and get it. And say goodbye to your mother. I haven't all day, you know.'

Alan was shocked when he saw his mother sitting at the table, her head in her elbow, her shoulders heaving. He felt a child's instant intuitive sympathy and fear for her sorrow, the sorrow of the source.

'What's wrong, Mum?'

She recovered quickly, took him in her arms. 'It's nothing, darling.' But she knew that wouldn't be enough. 'Well, sometimes adults cry when they think of their own parents. And you know my Daddy died last year, and I sometimes miss him. That's why I was crying, but I'm all right now. Seeing you looking so bright and bushy-tailed makes me feel better.' She kissed him. 'Hurry now, off to school.'

George drove in silence, except for an occasional curse at a truck in front of him that was moving with the speed of a bicycle. It was one of those tiny trucks called *Api*, or Bees, that infest Italian roads. They make a bee-like sound as they trundle along, and the effect this one had on George was up there with the annoyance a bee would cause him, buzzing around his balding head.

'Fucking wanker,' he muttered.

'What's a wanker?' Alan asked.

'Never mind. Have you done your homework?'

'I did my best. It was hard. Will you play with me after school today?'

'I can't. Too busy.'

'But Mum said you're not writing.'

'I'm busy with other matters.'

'Why do you never play with me, George?'

It was on the tip of George's tongue to say 'Because you're not my child', but he checked himself.

'Ask me to play with you in Italian, and I will.'

'I can't! It's not fair! You promised me.'

George felt a twinge of sympathy for the lonely child who had enough gumption to challenge him about his neglect of his surrogate fatherly duties, but he stifled it, especially seeing that this was a world where there were wankers driving around in contraptions called *Api* at a snail's pace, impeding all reasonable progress. A bit of loneliness would be the making of that child, he thought; force him back on his own resources, it would.

'Learn your Italian after school, get really stuck into it, and soon you'll have lots of other children to play with. Here we are. Out you get.'

Opening the car door, Alan was assailed by a Babel of children's screeching voices from the schoolyard. One boy saw him and shouted 'Ciao, Alan!', came over and took him by the hand into a maelstrom of swinging heads and limbs. That was Tommaso, a son of one of the landlord's friends. All they could say comprehensibly to one another at this stage was 'Ciao' and 'OK'.

In the classroom, doing drawings, Alan remembered his grandfather on a slab in the mortuary. His mother had brought him to say goodbye. His grandfather was there, and yet not there in some indescribable way, his face congealed in a silence which was not like George's bad moods, more like the silence of the woods. All day, as he played the new language game of *dai, dammela, tutti seduti, pastasciutta,* the shadow of the forest, which was also the shadow of his mother's crying, stood in the background, discreetly waiting for an answer.

George feared returning to the house and facing Barbara. And Barbara feared George's return to the house. For a whole week, they had managed to avoid the big issue that had exploded on the terrace of the town bar, and kept up an appearance of normality in front of Alan. But Barbara could no longer put up with the unspoken horror of what she saw as George's descent into lunacy, expert though he seemed to be at hiding it in public. George, on the other hand, could no longer accept Barbara's coldness towards him. He felt hugely resentful that she had not accepted reverently a happening which had bestowed on him a certain privileged access to the preternatural. George was like that: even when he washed a dish or two, he expected acknowledgement; almost as if he wasn't part of a family set-up, just a stranger who had come in and graciously cleaned a few dishes. And yet Barbara felt that she could not simply walk out on George, who had hinted darkly along the way of their relationship about the enormous baggage he was carrying. She had sensed it too, from the day they had first met, in the darkness that crossed his eyes. It was also in the little she had browsed of his writings, painful to read though presented as someone else's troubles. 'Bleak' was a word the critics had for his novel; 'unrelenting' was another, and 'excruciating' was an unkind third.

Still sitting at the table where she had kissed Alan off to school, Barbara decided to offer George a way out of the impasse: either he should make more sense or he should promise to see a psychiatrist. But in the car, which she now heard approaching laboriously up the dust road, George was thinking that Barbara would have to take him or leave him as he now was, because something ineluctable had entered his life.

As George got out of the car, Babs the Alsatian came up to him, all aquiver with excited greeting, probably hoping for a walk. George patted her perfunctorily – 'Not now, doggie, later' – and brushed past her up the steps.

'Be sure and ask Rogero what his position is on abortion,' a voice said. The goose-pimples stood up on George's neck. He wheeled around and saw Babs slinking away, disappointed with the brevity of their exchange – or was she guilty for being the mouthpiece of what had just been uttered?

George entered the kitchen. Barbara looked up and said 'Oh hello, George', offering a truce. He flopped down on a chair beside her, clasped her hand.

'The dog is talking to me,' he sobbed. 'The bloody Alsatian is talking to me.'

Suddenly a door clicked open in Barbara's mind, and a dark form entered her consciousness. There was something about the dogs.

'Don't worry, love,' she said, stroking George's tormented head, recognizing her own fear for the first time. 'We'll tackle this together, whatever it is.'

Originally things had been different between Barbara and Giorgio, but there was definitely something about the dogs. She had shared her son's enthusiasm for them: they had taken the dogs on long walks, and Barbara had even begun a series of 'doggy sketches', idly doodling dog faces on a pad as she and Alan rested on the steps of an abandoned house, while Giorgio, Babs and Carinosa hovered and panted around them, impa-tient to carry on. And she had developed a particular fascination for Giorgio, the mongrel with an unspecified percentage of Border Collie, whom the landlord told her had been badly abused by his former owner.

But even the most imperturbable of watercolourists have an Achilles heel, and Giorgio found a little crack in Barbara's nature, and stealthily burrowed, a little slippage of dusty earth at a time, until a sizeable hole had been made, and the painter, unbeknownst to herself, began to find excuses not to bring the dogs on walks, taking tortuous routes around the house to avoid them, much to Alan's disappointment.

Giorgio was slightly smaller than the Alsatian, but of a more amusing build, with a daintiness teetering on the ridiculous. He had delicately tapered legs and dainty buttocks that swayed coquettishly when he trotted. In an amusing, slightly ridiculous way, he was all of a piece: there seemed to be no joins in him at all when he ran, he was a kind of liquid dog, or rather a jelly dog with a very harmonious co-ordinated wobble. His paws were neatly defined; you could count his tarmacadam toes, and they each had a long nail in its proper place. He had an elegant ankle. The colour of his tiny dick also verged on tarmacadam, with an admixture of birthmark purple. Apart from that, he was a regulation black and white, more black on top and white beneath, and his insignificant member was hidden in a little tuft like white grass.

To Barbara, however, Giorgio's head and face presented a cubist conundrum of alternating planes and simultaneous perspectives. When every bit of him moved together, the head and face were part of the joke, and therefore posed no problem. She could have called him Mutt, if only the Alsatian, with whom he occasionally overlapped necks as they ran side by side, would ever consent to be called Jeff. But the Alsatian always kept a part of herself aloof, and wouldn't quite coalesce into the potential duo. And Giorgio remained a Mutt without Jeff, something that is not quite right. Potentially comic, he lacked a context to confirm that he was funny ha-ha and not funny peculiar.

The first aspect that Giorgio's face presented was a disturbingly innocent one. Innocence was all right where Barbara was concerned, as long as it exhibited staying power. Failing that, she could allow that there were certain acceptable ways of losing one's innocence: having sexual intercourse at an early age, abandoning one's belief in a just and merciful God, accepting bribes, betraying a friend, and so on. All these paths to the loss of innocence, however, presupposed a temporal progression: first there was innocence and then there was innocence no longer. Barbara, if pushed, might even admit to the possibility of a third state, the regaining of innocence, a state all the more admirable in that it is tempered by experience; this too of course involved a linear progression through time.

But Giorgio's innocence did not conform to this law. Giorgio continually lost and regained his innocence, even in the course of one day, in the same way that you might lose and find your car keys or your glasses. Giorgio's innocence was in there somewhere, and it sometimes came out, like the weather-house woman on warm sunny days. Sometimes he came running towards Barbara, his face almost human, childlike in its vulnerability, eager, fresh, bathed in a soft and gentle aura. But looking again, as he turned his head, she'd glimpse the saw-toothed grin without pity, the light of wickedness in the eyes, the beast waiting for famine and circumstance. Then she'd search agitatedly in the pockets of his face for the child-dog she had lost, and see the jackal Anubis, weighing her heart on the scales against the figure of Ma'at, in the presence of Osiris, on the day of her Last Judgement...

But all this is a joke, said Mutt the Comedian, as he butted her elbow repeatedly with his head, wanting to be rubbed or scratched or brought for a walk. Look for my innocence, it's a flurry of dust with a white tail, receding down the ochre road, with the woods and vineyards basking in the soft light of autumn, the pale blue smoke rising already from a nearby chimney. All is now and Giorgio, my Barbara of the many abandoned sketches, and the night of Anubis approaches.

Take me now, my Barbara, take me for a walk in the oak woods, where I will show you a secret place among the decaying mushrooms, in the silence of watching wild boars, before once and for all comes the night, in a clearing where the last shaft of sunlight illuminates my birthmark-purple member, be with me in Dante's *selva oscura*, where the path narrows and disappears on the edge of a fall, drink with me from the bitter cup of being neither this nor that, from the chalice of despised otherness. Watch me scrub away with demented paws my territorial markings, making our forest nook a place of nowhere in no time at all. And when the moon rises, I will sing for you, as my ancestors the jackals sung in that alternate light, enough to pull the human soul out of its body.

Alan had risen early. He was out feeding the geese and hens with Rogero, and receiving instructions on how to feed the dogs.

'You must be careful when you're feeding the doggies,' Rogero said.

Alan was scooping meal into a bucket, counting the scoops,

one, two, three, four, concentrating.

'I said you must be careful when you're feeding the dogs, Alan. You must make sure they all get the same amount.'

'What's *amount*?' Alan asked, as they came out of the shed into the bright cold morning.

'Well, if you give one bone to Giorgio, you must also give one to Babs, and one to Carinosa. Otherwise Babs and Carinosa will be cross; they won't like it.'

They went through a gate to the animals' enclosure. The geese and hens rushed forward. The geese honked *Baarrdal, Baarrdal,* flapping their big strong wings, frightening the hens out of their way. But the hens were adept at peck-and-run, at snatching a scrap at a time from under the big stupid geese. The goats were not involved in this scramble; they were at the other side of the enclosure, eating hay.

Alan held the bucket tightly; this was *his* job now. He scattered the grain indiscriminately. It was an important job; you could see its importance in the set of his shoulders. Rogero gently directed Alan. Random distribution was the answer to the power imbalance, because the geese moved more ponderously than the hens and made an enormous fuss of getting from one place to another.

'Babs and Giorgio are bigger than Carinosa,' Alan said when they were finished. 'They need more bones because they're bigger dogs.'

'So then you give a big bone to Giorgio, a big bone to Babs, and a small bone to Carinosa.'

'But Babs always finishes her bone first, and then she growls at Carinosa, and she gets frightened, and then Babs takes her bone.'

'I know. I know. Look. I have an idea. We'll feed the dogs together, just as we do the hens and geese. You keep the scraps until I come back in the evening. Alright?'

'OK. Babs is a funny name for a dog. George sometimes

calls my mum Babs, but she doesn't like it 'cos her real name is Barbara.'

'I see.'

Alan put the bucket back in the shed and Rogero locked the door.

'I must be off now. See you at doggy-feeding time. *A stasera.*' The landlord hurried off to wash and dress for work.

'*Ciao,*' the boy shouted to his departing back.

A long field, still white with frost in the shadow of the climbing trees, ran along the forest's edge. Alan turned round to look at this border of his world. There was a darkness among the trees that wasn't the same as night. There was something different about the trees, new spaces among them, shadowy pieces of emptiness. They gave off a ghostly aura. Light fell slantwise on the ridge of hills in great shafts; between the hills there were soft mysterious depths. Nothing moved, but he could hear the twittering of birds.

It was cold standing there, but so bright.

'Alan, school!'

'Coming, Mum!'

Good old Mum – she's driving me today. Not hobaril George. Big fatty. Why is it so quiet in the woods? Run, run, run. *A stasera.*

George sat in a wicker armchair in the middle of the steam-filled room, watching television, while Barbara cooked a spaghetti supper. Condensation blurred the windows and the glass in the door leading to the balcony. It was November, cold and foggy outside. Darkness had fallen at about five, and the dogs were restless. For the past hour or so, they had barked at anything that sounded through the fog's stillness, even at the occasional creak of the chain by which the Aladdin's lamp dangled from a privet tree. Is that the squeaking of a shoe? Woof, woof, arf arf. Here we go again.

Giorgio's bark had sometimes modulated into a howl which upset Barbara so much that she became accident-prone, dropping tomatoes on the floor, hurting her side against a table edge. Ever since her dog-phobia had entered her waking life, she hadn't been able to tell George about it. She wasn't sure why she couldn't; she had mixed, uncertain motives for keeping it concealed. It was unthinkable that a couple should develop psychiatric problems simultaneously. She also thought that George's condition was worse than hers, and that if she were to confirm his sense of the abnormal and uncanny in their midst, he might feel licensed to let go completely. But there was another factor: she had a strong intuition to hold back, for some compelling reason that she could not quite grasp – something to do with herself alone, her own well-being. And so she acted as if everything was normal, and laboured emotionally at being breezy and positive, while George descended into a stupor, seemingly undisturbed by any further manifestations from the dark side. And the more George stupefied, the more Barbara felt she ought to keep up the charade of nurse-like good cheer. And the more winter made inroads, the more she feared Giorgio, the dog who howled by day and who laughed a wolf-laugh in her dreams, with long rows of saliva-dripping teeth.

George sat waiting for his supper, watching the three-day weather forecast, which showed masses of cloud rotating around Italy, with Italy for the most part in the clear, its only problem being the *nebbia*, the morning and evening fog so characteristic of November. Eventually, the clouds cleared over the rest of mainland Europe, and over the south of England. He was grimly satisfied to see, at the end of the forecast, that the heavy grey blanket still sat immoveable on Ireland.

'As it was in the beginning, is now, and ever shall be, cloud without end, Amen,' George intoned.

'You're a bit beforehand with grace, George,' Barbara said, attempting jollity. 'Pass me the plates, please.'

She dished out three portions of spaghetti with ragout while George held the plates.

'Alan,' shouted Barbara, 'supper's ready.'

The boy came out, looked at the spaghetti and said, 'Not spaghetti again. I had three plates of it in school for lunch.'

'Well the sauce in this one's different,' said Barbara. 'Eat up now.'

They sat around the table, George shovelling the food into his mouth, Alan toying with his, Barbara rolling hers carefully on her fork.

'What's *campione*?' asked Alan.

'It means champion,' George said. 'Why?'

'That's what they were calling me after lunch – *il campione*.'

'Did anyone else eat three plates of spaghetti?'

'No. Christian had two and a half, but he got sick.'

George laughed heartily for the first time since the Alsatian had smoked her roll-up. 'You're the champion spaghetti eater! What do you think of that, Barbara? After a couple of months he can beat the Italians at eating spaghetti.'

'Mind you don't get sick, darling,' she cautioned. 'I don't think it's a good way of making friends, showing off how much you can eat.'

'I'll get sick if I eat any more spaghetti,' declared Alan, pushing away his plate. 'Can I have some ice cream?'

'All right, just this time.'

Alan went to the fridge and took out a box of cones from the freezer compartment.

'Do they always have spaghetti for school lunch?' George asked.

'No. They have all kinds of things. Some are yukky, others are nice – like *callellony*.'

'*Cannellone*,' corrected George.

'*Callellony*. George can I play Snake on your computer?'

'Off you go.' Alan went back to his bedroom with two ice-cream cones.

Not as much as taking his plate to the sink, George returned to his armchair and zapped the television until he found a soccer match. Barbara watched him. A feeling of angry desperation swept over her. Suddenly she rose and walked across the room to him.

'Turn off that fucking television!' she grinded into his eardrum.

Startled, George dropped the remote control. Its batteries rolled across the floor. Barbara pressed the button on the set: darkness swallowed a pleasant evening of Perugia vs AC Milan, offering instead *more of the same*, as George thought, mustering his willpower to weather another storm.

'What's wrong now?' he said, a little shocked and sheepish.

'What isn't wrong?'

They stood facing one another, the dark mute television acting as an umpire between them.

'Well, I thought things were OK. I thought you were quite cheerful about the present set-up.'

'What set-up? There isn't any set-up, George. You have better Italian than me, and you can't even be bothered to ask at the school is there some kind of regular weekly menu, just to make sure Alan won't have spaghetti coming out of his ears by Christmas.'

'Oh is that it? Sorry. I'll ask tomorrow.'

'Don't bother, George. It's too late. Our great plan is in a mess. Look at you, you're just pigging out the year, a couch potato. You won't lift a finger. You won't do anything. And, above all, we've been here two and a half months and we haven't met a soul, we haven't a friend to come to visit us or to go and see…'

'What do you expect? I came here with a list of contacts

as long as my arm, but you wouldn't let me bring my cellphone to ring them, because we're supposed to be back in a state of Rousseauesque innocence, writing bloody letters. And we haven't got an extension in the apartment, so every time we want to make a call, it's an expedition downstairs to *their* phone, with many apologies, that is if they're in, and then having to leave a message. And they may not even tell us if anyone replied. It's no wonder we have no one – '

'Excuses as usual, George. You've all day at your disposal, and a car. You could go to the post office and phone from there. But you're too fucking lazy and lethargic. It's a nightmare. We've nowhere to go, we don't even exist as far as anyone is concerned, the only conversations we have are about technicalities with the landlord and *grazie, buon giorno, arrivederci* to teachers and shopkeepers...'

A furious scratching noise distracted them. They looked towards the source and saw the Alsatian through the glass panel of the door, standing on her hind legs, pawing the glass frantically, her tongue out, panting. Then they heard a voice: 'Down, Babs, down...' The Alsatian disappeared and was replaced by the gaunt figure of the landlord, sharp-featured, trimly white-bearded, tapping the pane.

George gathered himself and went to admit the surprise visitor.

Rogero was wearing a dark suit and dickeybowed shirt, and smiled as he looked perfunctorily at George, more lingeringly at Barbara, then around the room.

'Good evening. I see you've eaten already. I was going to invite you to supper. I'm having some friends over and it occurred to me you might like to meet them. They're quite interesting and speak reasonable English. Perhaps you could come down later for dessert and drinks? Tessa has made a scrumptious tiramisu. She makes her own mascarpone. What do you think?'

Barbara and George looked at one another, and saw the astonishment in one another's eyes. Somehow Barbara managed to stammer, 'It's so kind of you. Thanks very much.'

'Well, see you about ten, then,' said Rogero smilingly, leavingly.

'A pity the Marchesa had to leave so early,' Rogero said to Barbara. 'She's something of a local historian as well as being gentry, and knows a great deal about the place. She has some particularly hair-raising stories about goings-on in this very valley. Anyway, she's invited us all to a *spaghettata* on Boxing Day. She'll fill you in then.'

'What's a *spaghettata*?' Barbara asked.

'Well, as the name suggests, it's a meal with spaghetti.'

'My Italian is so poor. I have no confidence. I knew the word had something to do with spaghetti. But when you said it, it sounded very anarchic and energetic, and I had this image of people flinging spaghetti all over the place, a spaghetti fight – like a pillow fight.' Barbara giggled.

Rogero laughed. 'Oh dear no. I don't think the Marchesa would be up for that kind of behaviour at all.'

'She seems rather self-contained.'

'Yes. Haughty and removed in a well-mannered way. She takes her Marchesa-ship seriously, and is quite medieval for all her modern façade. The *spaghettata*, of course, is a case in point. We won't get invited to a proper *cena*. She really caught me out tonight, coming in jeans and jumper. It's her way of saying that she's slumming. The Marchesa doesn't travel well; she's happier receiving vassals in the villa. Look at this apartment' – Rogero waved his arms around – 'the low ceilings, the room long and narrow. What she was probably thinking is *The animals used to be stabled here*. And her nose is so refined, she could probably still smell them.'

'Oh dear,' tittered Barbara, 'she sounds like a bit of a snob. And her husband is excessively quiet.'

'Don't be deceived, my dear. He's terribly capable. He's both an engineer and an architect. He restored the villa almost single-handedly. But enough of the gentry. How are you settling in here?'

'Oh very well,' Barbara lied. 'It's a lovely place. Very secluded and peaceful.'

'It can be too quiet. You need to get about a bit more. That's what I said to myself tonight: why not ask them down to meet a few people? The Italians are strange. They'll either take to you completely or not at all. But you must jump in and take your chances with them...'

The Marchesa had departed shortly after dessert, taking her excessively quiet but extremely capable husband with her, creating a gap in the seating arrangements, which left George islanded with Tessa, and Barbara with Rogero, each pair on their second bottle of Montefalco. Every now and then, Barbara would glance over at George, and Tessa would glance over at Rogero. But Rogero failed to take his eyes off Barbara, and George's roved incessantly up and down the contours of Tessa, a stunning twenty-something who, despite the time of year, was wearing very little, although she had come to the soirée in an enormous black fur coat. Tessa's face was marred somewhat by a swollen bruise around her left eye.

'That's a real shiner you've got there,' George remarked.

'Excuse me, what is this *shainer* you are saying?'

'A black eye. The bruising all around your left eye.' George took the opportunity to touch her cheek.

Tessa laughed huskily. '*Bleck aye.* Yesterday I bump into a stupid door when I was cleaning my kitchen. The doctor he say it goes soon. Then I am beautiful again. No more *blek aye.*' Another husky laugh, and George watched her breasts shake.

Only a narrow table stood between George and the object of his desire. He could hardly restrain himself from reaching across it and groping her. Easy now, he thought to himself. Civilized soirée here. Keep the conversation going.

'That was the nicest tiramisu I have ever tasted,' he declared. 'It certainly picked me up.'

'Thenk you,' beamed Tessa. 'But what is *peeked me up*?'

'That's the English for tiramisu. Pick me up. Make me happy.'

'I like to make people happy.' The happy-making breasts shook again. Then Tessa became serious, confiding, as George poured two more glasses of wine. 'Rogero not happy.' She said this in a low voice, glancing furtively across to make sure the landlord was still deep in conversation with his female tenant. She needn't have worried.

A slight sourness crept into George's lust. So now we must discuss the well-being of that creep, he thought. But he smiled a fake interest: 'Really?'

'Really. He really is so unhappy. He only is happy when his wife is gone. She is not well – *é pazza*.' Tessa put a finger to her temple. 'Sometime she must go to hospital for a little while. Like now. But I am saying too much.'

Outside, in the damp clinging cold, Giorgio erupted in a fit of barking. A moment later the three dogs were creating a disturbance. And out of the harsh, clashing discord, the random intermingling of hoarse barks and hollow barks and whiplash yelps, always expected yet full of terror when it came, soared the free continuous rising wail of supernatural misery, sending a shiver up Barbara's spine, goosing her neck. For a split second, George saw the Alsatian sitting across the table instead of Tessa. He took an enormous gulp of wine, drained his glass.

'Bravo!' enthused Tessa and laughed breast-shakingly. She was back again.

Noticing Barbara's discomfiture, Rogero rose and placing his hand on her bare shoulder murmured: 'Oh dear, I see you're upset by the dogs. Their convulsions can be very unexpected. Excuse me a moment.' He went out.

'Well, George,' said Barbara into the awkward silence. 'I can see you're enjoying yourself. Are you grooming her for a little spot of nooky then?'

'You don't seem to be doing too badly yourself,' George retorted.

'What is this *nooky*?' Tessa asked, uncertain what was going on, aware of the discordant note.

'You must be very cold, my dear,' sniped Barbara.

'No, I am not *colt*. I am always very hot.'

'You can say that again.'

Rogero returned, having temporarily pacified the mutts.

'It's the truffle wars,' he explained. 'Someone is out laying poison in this part of the forest. I'll have to quarantine the dogs. No more walkies for a while, I'm afraid.'

Barbara went to see if Alan was all right, kissed him and tucked in his scattered bedclothes. When she came back to the living room, George was sitting on the fouton, drinking a grappa. He motioned Barbara to come and sit beside him, a gesture towards reconciliation. Barbara stayed standing near the door to the bedroom.

'I was just testing the waters,' said George, answering the unspoken question. 'It's nice to know that one is still attractive at my age.'

'She's a flirt. She was leading you a merry chase. It was you who had the hots for *her*, not the other way round.'

'Well you weren't exactly all coy with your man.'

'We had a pleasant conversation, and he seemed much

nicer than I'd originally thought. That's all. I suppose I should be happy we've finally had a social evening. And I suppose I should also be happy that your drooling over that human tiramisu has made it so abundantly clear that you haven't become totally gay.'

'Ouch!' winced George, pouring himself another grappa. 'Nobody's one hundred per cent anything. Some people fuck animals.' He thought again of how Tessa had briefly become the Alsatian. What if she is the Alsatian? Then he said aloud, elliptically, 'That's why I'm drinking. To drown it all out.'

'Why do you never have the hots for me any more, George?'

'I do, right now,' he said eagerly. 'Can't we go to bed?' He got up, walked over and put his arms around her.

'You want me to be Tessa for the night, don't you?'

'Why not? I could kiss the bruise around your eye better, and as a reward for my kindness, you could kiss my dick bigger.'

Barbara couldn't help laughing, but disengaged herself from George's grasp. 'Nice try, but you're too drunk. And you're going to snore. Would you mind awfully sleeping on the fouton?'

'Aw, Barbara…'

'Goodnight, George.'

Next morning, Barbara and George lay half-awake thinking their different thoughts in their separate sleeping berths, she in the big bed with wrought-iron bedsteads, he scrunched up on the untransformed fouton that smelled of spilled grappa.

Barbara was thinking: why is there nothing in George's head but resentment, anger and obsessions? Why is he so remote and disengaged? And why do I still care? And why, ever since I came here, am I using foul language more than I ever did? And why am I afraid of the dogs? To dispel her anxieties, she recalled how pleasant Rogero had been the night before, and her anxieties went away and came back at her from another angle: why, why, why does that big remote angry obsessive head lack the slightest grip on reality? And why do I still care? And what's happening to my painting?

And George was thinking: what a strange coincidence that just as Barbara was building up to a full-scale tirade about her isolation in this place, who should appear but the Alsatian, pawing the door frantically, as much as to say *Hang on, there's help on the way, here comes company.* And was this arranged by whatever power resides in the field? Was it to keep Barbara tolerably sweet, so that I can continue my watchmanship without the distraction of lovers' disharmony? *Ah begod and it was, 'twas all that and more*, said the voice in his head. *Take things handy now. You'll know soon enough.*

The dogs were not quarantined. Instead, they were temporarily removed to fresh woods and pastures new. Rogero brought them to a friend's house in the southern part of the province. The man had his own woods and truffle wars, but an uneasy truce obtained in the region. Meanwhile the police, with more competent dogs than the exiled trio, combed the woods around Rogero's house for the poison, while the usual suspects sat in the town bars, unimpeded in their card-playing concentration by any fears of arrest, resolved to put down fresh poison as soon as the police had gone.

The absence of the dogs was the occasion when Barbara took her first steps towards greatness. These were steps taken unaccompanied into the woods, carrying acrylic pens, lead pencils and a sketchpad in a cloth bag. She felt the fear but still set off. No dogs of ambiguous protective qualities tailed her on these excursions. Instead, she had dropped into the cloth bag, among the art materials, a pepper spray she had always carried around in her handbag back in London. The landlord had told her to be wary of the Sardinian shepherds who minded their sheep on the hills, made pecorino cheese, and slept in the open or in abandoned homesteads. And so her ears were constantly alert for the tinkling of sheep-bells. But she confronted her fear of the woods and, entering them, confronted her fear of Giorgio in particular and of dogs in general, and found that it was the same as her fear of the woods and all her fears.

Finding a suitable rock or stump to sit on, she peered into the twilight among the trees, and steeled her heart not to quake. She sketched tree-trunks and bits of decaying wood in which Giorgio heads appeared, bosky nostrils and timbery teeth, knots for eyes. Giorgio, Babs and Carinosa creatures took shape in the twilight among the trees, but she remained seated and sketched them. Childe Rolande to the Dark Tower came, and felt the frightening good of it. In the dogs' absence, she confronted her fear in their arboreal counterparts, rated her anxiety on a scale of nought to ten as she worked, brought it down from ten to seven, from nine to four, from eight to two. She faced the ambivalence of her shadow self, and began to discern a faint and growing luminosity around its edge. Something bright within her was hiding behind the shadow.

That was after she had laid down a strong marker for George. It happened on one of the days following Rogero's soirée, when she had returned from delivering Alan to school.

'I'm going,' she said to George who was sprawled on the fouton, smelling of grappa.

George opened an eye. 'Where?'

She was standing at the door, bag in hand.

'I'm off to do some sketches. And not just for an hour. You can do the housework and prepare the dinner from now on.'

Housework was the sum of all George's fears. The way pasta sauce clung stubbornly to a fork he was washing, for instance, so that he had to scrape it off with his fingernails. The way he'd hoover the floor and find that he was only rearranging the dirt, because the bloody hoover was useless and technology hadn't solved the problem of cleaning, only made it more vexatious with a false promise of labour-saving. The way the flex of the machine got entangled in his legs. He sprung from the futon.

'That's not fair! We agreed to share it.'

'If you do it till the end of January, that'll be fair, because you haven't done a tap since we arrived,' Barbara said, then continued in a mock breezy tone. 'You can take a break every now and then to see how your field is getting on. Don't forget to make Alan's bed. And the place needs a good dusting. You will be sure to tell me of any revelations, won't you?' And she was gone.

George looked at the previous night's dishes: the remains of Barbara's supper, a brave attempt at a cannelloni bake, festering in a casserole dish; three forks, three plates, three glasses; a salad bowl with a few limp leaves of Lola Rossa lettuce clinging to the rim. He knew that this was where he should start; at least get the dishes done.

George hated housework because he was simultaneously lazy and obsessive. Looking at the dishes brought on a sense of terminal banality, a boredom so profound and malign that he felt as if an incubus had descended on his spirit and was slowly suffocating it, taking the life out of his existence, leaving him an existence without life or spirit. On the other hand, he knew that whenever he summoned his willpower to get started on any kind of household chore, he took ages doing it: in this case, the dishes could take him a good hour, few as they were. He would not be able to leave the glasses alone until they gleamed without fingerprint or other smudge when held up to the light. The forks, with starch lodged between the prongs, would be subjected to a series of minute inspections until the last tiny trace of the gunge had been teased out.

It seemed a simple task to start with: at least get the dishes out of the way, annul their hostile presence on the edge of the sink. George felt the incubus biting into his spirit, sucking the ichor away. He couldn't bear to look at the dishes: it was too much to ask. He went outside, and immediately felt better.

It was the beginning of December, a spell of soft, hazy sunshine, the trees of the forest mottled with the browns and yellows of autumn, holding on to their foliage in the still air. The leaves would all go, the landlord had said, in the first stiff wind. But they were holding on, under that enormous sky, cloud-crossed but not overcast, as day followed day towards the Feast of Christmas. It is good to be alive, thought George; the dishes belonged to a past he had escaped from.

The leaves of the oaks that flanked the house, between the landlord's patio and the slope that fell to the valley bottom, were only half-touched by light, not saturated; they were lanterns with their own soft internal glow, and their clusters around branches rested with a faint sense of the delicate equilibrium of uncoiled springs. Everything was silent; no dogs to create a racket as soon as he appeared. George hoped the dogs would never return; that they might perhaps be poisoned in a fresh outbreak of that other truffle war in the southern part of the province. And then the field shouted at him.

The idea of a shouting field isn't all that unusual. Many people have the experience that something in the landscape has suddenly shouted at them. A person may turn and their eyes are hit by a row of poplars in the distance: something about the trees has cried *Look at us, we're significant!* With eyes searching deeper for the significance, however, the person will find nothing, and so turn away and continue his journey a little puzzled, asking himself *What was it about that particular configuration of landscape – what was it that shouted at me?*

With George, it was different. The field shouted at him because he had entertained a bad thought about the dogs. It was too coincidental to be a coincidence. Peering through the gaps in the clusters of oak leaves, he had caught a glimpse of the field, just as he was wishing ill on the dogs, and the field had shouted at him. The cry was a kind of pulse, from bright to dark, to bright again to dark once more. He waited, watching for something else to happen. The sunlight rested faintly on the blurred green of the grass, and the stains of coarser growth were confused with the long shadows of clouds.

In the absence of anything substantially forthcoming from the powers that governed the field, George eventually gave up watching and waiting, turned his thoughts towards his publisher, and went to town to collect the post. There was no delivery to the rural areas, so the couple had rented a mailbox at the post office.

Before George left for Italy, there had been rancour about his novel. The publisher had told him it wasn't selling well, and George had retorted that the publisher had done little to publicize or distribute the book. The press was a rather small operation in Dublin, and the publisher was busy writing and placing a novel of his own at the time George's came out. The imprint received an annual grant from the Arts Council for publishing 'works of literary merit'. This grant enabled the publisher to pay his production costs, but there was very little of it left for promotion and distribution. George was expected, in these circumstances, to be his own publicist and also to help with the distribution. The publisher told him so, and George had expressed the unreasonable but strong view that the publisher was a charlatan and a wanker, and had stomped off, bitterly disappointed, his dreams of bestsellerdom in tatters.

And yet he had continued to hope that his novel was a slow burner and had picked up since he had come to Italy, and that his publisher, being a businessman as well as a competing author, would forget the rancour, regret that he had let a writer go who was beginning to show a profit, and send George a letter of entreaty: *Come back, all is forgiven, new horizons beckon, fame and fortune await you, a book signing tour of all the major cities in Ireland and Britain is our immediate priority, enclosed please find cheque for substantial royalties.*

There was an entire wall of numbered mail boxes on either side of the post office door. George stood for a few minutes in front of his box, plucking up the resolution to put a brave face on it if there wasn't a letter from his publisher. He felt in his pocket for the key, took a deep breath and opened No. 26. His box was on the second lowest row, about two feet above the ground, and the search for letters was strenuous to his unfit body: a breath-extinguishing squat, followed by much gasping for air, then a blind groping with fingers for the touch of paper, causing more stretch and strain. The box was really a shaft, because the mail was inserted from inside the post office, where there was a grid of openings which mirrored the outside ones.

George's fingers touched paper, felt around it, defined it as a single item. He pulled it out to the light. Still on his hunkers – it was as difficult to get back up as it was to get down – he beheld an ordinary elongated brown business envelope with an Irish stamp. With the energy of dawning promise, he stood erect. He brought the letter round to brighter light, peered at the postmark: *Baile Átha Cliath*. It had been redirected from his former address in London.

He couldn't keep himself from opening it immediately, in front of the post office, with a steady flow of people going in and out past him, figures attending to the annual ritual of sending festive greetings to far-flung friends and relatives. This letter was surely from his repentant publisher.

He pulled out the contents: two pieces of paper stapled together. The top one was a complimentary slip, not a letter, though it was indeed from his publisher. Underneath the printed *With Compliments from Hurdlesford Press* was written in biro *Cheque for outstanding royalties.* His heart thumping, George turned over the complimentary slip to look at the cheque. It was for the amount of €6.66.

In shock, he dropped the stapled slips of paper and they wafted down the street. A passing woman picked them up and handed them back to him. 'Prego, Signore.' Mechanically, he accepted them, and immediately realised that this was the way with written spells or curses: you're allowed one chance to get rid of them, but if you don't succeed, if they somehow come back to you, it's for keeps.

A very disturbed George drove back hastily to what he now considered the sheer sanity of washing dishes, the sound humility of dusting, the sober, gurgling contentment of the laundry room, the serene banality of cooking.

Fortunately or unfortunately, he didn't reach his secure and salutary destination right away. His red Toyota turned off the highway at a wooden sign on which were painted the words *Ai Poderi* – To the Farms. The car wound its way along the narrow dusty white road, over the little humpbacked bridge, up the hill past the enormous ruined mansion which Barbara called Wuthering Heights, turned sharp left, passed an olive grove, and came to a sudden screeching stop a hundred meters before Rogero's place – right beside the field.

Years later, George would tell the one person who was prepared to listen that he wasn't sure whether he had braked because of a drainage channel crossing the road's soft surface, or the car had stopped of its own accord. It would have been unusual for him to break because of a drainage channel, however deep: he was a reckless and impatient driver. George would then go on to inform his listener that what he saw in the field that afternoon was the beginning of the end – the end, that is, of his old life. Indulging an extent of mental convolution, he then explained how it was also the end of the beginning, because the beginning of the beginning was his actual arrival in that haunted rural recess of Italy, and what he saw in the field that day was the end of the beginning in the sense of being a substantial supernatural clue as to what the place was doing to him, with him, for him and against him, the most detailed of a series of teasingly obscure hints that up to then did not give rise to anything except a general feeling of the uncanny and a premonition of more to come.

Halted there, George became aware of a flurry of activity in the corner of his eye. When he looked through the side-window, everything in the field went dark. It was moonlit night, and shadows were rushing around on the grass. They could have been animals, and at one stage it seemed that the three exiled dogs were careering around at the head of the other shadow-creatures. Everything kept changing. Up above was a moon that looked like an enormous egg in a dark eggcup. The shadows grew more frenetic and coalesced into a big ball that rolled to and fro, from one end of the field to the other. The ball flattened out and rose again as a circle of upright shadows, motionless now, with spaces between them. They solidified into a circle of standing stones. One shadow remained pulsing in the centre of the circle. It slowly grew bright and formed the shape of a boy. There was the sheen of a boy's body, naked under the moon, in the centre of the circle of standing stones. The boy was kneeling, his head drooped, his arms limp in an attitude of despair or grief. And George felt that he knew the boy, but could not remember him.

Then a figure stepped out from behind one of the standing stones, a man in a long black garment and black beret, who went up to the boy, pulled him to his feet and blindfolded him. And at once George knew: *the boy is not to see; he must not see the others who are coming.* And then the shadows all moved and twisted around and became an enormous ball and flew up into the moon.

It was day again, late afternoon, and the field was still except for the nodding of the wild chicory flowers: *Oh yes, oh yes, it happened; believe us, we who are about to die.*

The Policlinico, on one of the city's satellite hills, was entered through an imposing arch which was a bottleneck for traffic. A hospital orderly sweated in the middle of the street outside this noble portal, trying to divert cars back around the piazza to the small car park on the other side. It didn't help that the car park was already full, and that a two-tailed queue obtruded from it into the through traffic. The orderly's gesticulations were frenzied, his voice hoarse from shouting at the incredibly large percentage of the sick and their relatives who felt that now was the time to make an issue of their God-given right to a parking space inside the grounds. Horns honked, hundreds of engines throbbed together at a standstill, windows were lowered, heads craned out to shout the most appalling blasphemies and the most damning of curses at the unfortunate functionary. He appealed in vain that the inner area was *completa – completa – completa*, then lost his temper once more at the stupidity of these anxious invalids and their arrogant entourages with regard to the crassly obvious fact that not another single vehicle could fit in the hospital grounds.

'They are parking on the rose bushes in there,' he roared

at one driver. 'They are parking on the statue of Padre Pio, they are parking in the waiting rooms, they are parking on the roof.' He gesticulated upwards with both hands, then inwards towards his chest. 'What do you expect me to do?'

'*Vai fotterti*! Go and fuck yourself!' shouted an old man in the passenger seat, raising his walking stick and gesturing obscenely with it across the driver's face.

That was it. The attendant walked away. A quarter of an hour later the police arrived and erected a barrier across the archway.

Barbara, glad she had come by bus, watched this demonstration of Italian chaos and road-temper with bitter satisfaction. It could never happen in Britain, where they calmly cooked their lunches on little primus stoves on the bonnets of their cars in tailbacks to Folkestone and Brighton. Welcome to Italy, she thought ironically, remembering that she had said it to George when he had been tetchy in the Autoservizio on their very first day in the country, the Day of the Hundred Tunnels.

She only half-believed that Britain was the best, the most civilized country in the world. But it was on occasions like this that she wished she was back home. She had already booked one appointment in the wrong clinic; a wasted journey, a wasted bus fare, a wasted morning. Only at the Policlinico could they do the blood test for her thyroid complaint. The fact that in the Policlinico they analysed samples with a degree of accuracy hitherto unknown, by techniques of nuclear medicine, did not impress Barbara. What would remain with her was the impression created by all the regional functionaries she had encountered over the previous three weeks – that her case was difficult, bordering on the impossible; and yet all she had asked for was a simple blood test.

Barbara's casual relationship with the Italian language hadn't, of course, helped matters. After an initial enthusiasm with tape and textbook, she had lost interest. And she still couldn't quite grasp why these minions of administrative paralysis did not speak her world-wide native tongue. Specimens who were said to speak English had been paraded before her, but it had soon become plain that their vocabulary didn't extend much beyond *OK* and *No problem*. How else was it that a fifteen-minute speech, delivered in a tone of sympathetic regret, could translate so briefly, and positively, into English? But when these polyglots had been removed to the wings, the situation remained the same: the *esame di sangue* cannot be done here, it must be done at the Policlinico; no, we cannot make an *appuntamento* for you from here; no, you cannot make one by phone, *non si può*; first you must go to the Policlinico to make your appointment, and then you must go back there to make your blood test.

When she walked under the arch, Barbara found herself in a hospital city. The road led round in a huge circle from one department to another, with signposted by-roads to left and right. Directly opposite the arch was a building that looked like a town hall, and behind it an old church which probably harboured a fresco or two by Piero della Francesco or Pietro Vannucci, as did most of the churches in the region. There were a couple of cafés, a restaurant, a bank with an ATM, and other amenities. It was a city of the sick, and the sick swarmed on the thoroughfares, woebegone, with their visitors; some were in their dressing gowns in the mid-December mildness. It seemed to Barbara that this city was a parody of the healthy city on the higher hill above; the two composed a Dantesque parable of heaven and hell. Cars were parked all along the main roads and up the by-roads. There was a constant movement of ambulances and other hospital vehicles, of cars leaving, and now, again, of cars entering. The chaos outside had been cleared and the orderly was back in front of the arch, applying with renewed determination the principle that one may enter for every one that leaves.

Barbara could not find the Department of Nuclear Medicine. Two green-jacketed medics came out of a building as she passed, each holding a plastic bucket marked *Infetto*: plague carriers. She plucked up the courage to ask directions.

'Scusi, dove Medicine Nucleare?'

The older of the men, baldingly grey-haired, understood her accent to import a calling upon his mimetic resources.

'Questa via,' he enunciated, pointing back the way she had come. 'Trecento metri.' Here he held up three fingers and performed a vigorous little dance to convey meters. 'Dopo la banca, capito?' Here he rubbed his thumb against two fingers to signify banknotes.

'Gratseeay,' Barbara said and turned back towards the bank, mortified that the man had felt the need to use sign-language even for the word *banca*.

As she sat in the waiting corridor, holding a little piece of cardboard with the number 21 written on it in biro, and wishing it had been her age, she was intrigued to notice that many of the people there had not arrived for blood tests, but were relatives or friends who came to support and comfort. A middle-aged woman stood outside the sample room, talking jokily to her companion inside, an elderly man undergoing the needle. But the ones who had numbered pieces of cardboard all looked nervous: number 7 was a young woman who sat biting her nails, and number 16 a tall shabbily suited youth who paced the corridor, his cardboard held in a palm which he kept opening and closing.

Barbara wondered whether these people were nervous of the needle or of the result of the blood test. Perhaps of both. Or maybe above all they were nervous of being in this city of the sick, and wanted to get back as soon as possible to the city of health above. You could go back to the disease-oblivious city only if your sickness was moderate; everyone harbours the dread of being imprisoned by serious illness in such a place as this. She remembered how her father had refused to go to hospital, even for tests. 'Stay away from hospitals and doctors,' he used to say. 'They'll kill you.'

Her own thyroid problem had been under control for some years now, but ironically, just before she left for Italy, something had gone amiss with her blood figures. The thyroid-stimulating hormone had decreased its activity, and even though the other figures were within the normal range, this decrease usually harbingered an imminent increase in thyroxin levels. The thyroid-stimulating hormone was a kind of prophetic entity: somehow, like birds deserting an island well before the arrival of a tsunami, it knew the future. Her specialist had told her to have another blood test after three months, and if the thyroxin had risen above the acceptable levels, to come back to London for a consultation.

She shuddered to remember what had happened to her feelings one awful day when her sickness was well advanced without her knowing it. She couldn't feel the love she had always felt for Alan; nothing but an uncontrollable arid lack of affection that brought with it an existential sense of terror, as if aliens were dehumanising her by remote control. She wanted to scream and break things, or run out into the traffic, tear off the Nessus shirt of her skin, jump from a roof, anything to escape that demonic aridity. Now she recognised that her body had been trying to tell her something that day: *Look after me because I'm sick; put first things first.* Her body had been closing in on itself, shutting out everything else.

Her specialist had been confident, however, about her going to Italy. There were little anomalies that occurred every now and then; and besides, the thyroid levels were still respectable. Ever since the consultation, she had been observing herself for the classic symptoms – sweats, weight loss, palpitations, exhaustion – but they hadn't shown. Well, maybe occasional palpitations and perspiring during a strenuous walk;

but, if anything, she was filling out a bit despite all the exercise. She did, of course, sleep a lot.

She thought of George, wondered if his crazy obsessions could be the result of an overactive gland. She could forgive his idiocy more readily if that were the case. She was tired of his self-absorption, his transparent lack of interest in her. Her sickness was taboo to George. He was annoyed if she even mentioned it; he had refused to go with her to any of her bureaucratic encounters, even though his command of the language was much better than hers.

On the positive side, though, he had actually begun to do some housework in the past week; not much, but enough to show that her annoyance had registered, enough to give her some satisfaction in her new-found assertiveness and authority, to stave off her threatened exit. But she still wasn't sure whether or not she'd go home for Christmas. She felt she ought to for her widowed mother's sake. But now that she was beginning to confront her fears, and her painting was changing, maybe she should stay. The new style of painting she was developing responded better to acrylics than to water colours. The dogs were returning soon from the south of the province. That would surely be a big test of her mettle...

Her number was called. A cosy plump nurse with glasses and a radiant smile took her blood sample. She felt the prick of the needle, watched her blood surge into the syringe. She held a wad of cotton to the wound while the nurse labelled the sample. A little strip of plaster with two white eyes was placed over the pierced flesh, and the ordeal was over.

She left the hospital, past the dense but smooth-flowing traffic. A different orderly was now on point duty. She walked up narrow streets, up flights of steps, stood on the elevator, the *scala mobile*, that bore her towards the City of Light. Suddenly she was determined to do something sociable. She would invite Rogero and his wife to a dinner party, just before Christmas, along with the Marchesa and her husband. But not Tessa. She would ask Rogero to invite a few others as well on her behalf.

There was also the matter of presents. What would she buy for George, who ploughed the lonely furrow of his prophetic field? She laughed out loud at the answer that came immediately to mind, so that people passing on the down elevator stared at her curiously. She would buy George one of those crystal balls with snow in them, a crystal ball with nothing else inside – no mansion, no mountains, no Virgin and Child, no Santa Claus with sled and reindeers. A crystal ball with nothing in it but snow.

And then she cried.

George needed a whiskey, or failing that a Vecchia Romagna, because he was under pressure. Barbara was holding a dinner party that very evening. She had decided to go home for Christmas, and was determined to go out with a sociable bang. She would return only if George continued to improve, and she would be particularly impressed if he made a Herculean effort today to help out, and be pleasant to the guests. He had been sent to town for some seasoning necessary for a recipe, and already he couldn't recall what it was. Rosemary? It couldn't be rosemary because there were hedges of it around the landlord's house. He decided that it must be fennel, and bought a bulb of it at the Ortofrutta's, then went to the post office to see if there were any Christmas cards from home.

There hadn't been any post for him, which lowered his already profoundly low self-esteem and increased his craving for a drink. He was walking from the post office, heading up a narrow alley towards the main street and the most anonymous bar in town, namely the biggest, where he could hide away in a corner for a few hours, nurse his wounded feelings with alcohol, and not have to go home to face Barbara, pretend to be helpful, come up with inane suggestions that would provoke sarcastic responses, and stand his ground long enough for her to think he was on the mend, so that even though he had to face Christmas alone he could at least phone her, and maybe even bask in the absence that makes the heart grow fonder at the other end of the line a thousand miles away. He ought to go back and face a day of domestic labour with Barbara in her bossy mode, but he wasn't up to it – not yet.

It was the day of the winter solstice, and he remembered the poem by John Donne that begins *'Tis the year's midnight, and it is the day's...* The year's midnight, this day; how apt, he ruminated, how well it fits with my confusion and despair: my year in Italy has already reached its midnight. *Lucy's, who scarce seven hours herself unmasks...* St Lucy's Day used to be the shortest by tradition, but modern meteorology had done away with this venerable meshing of saint's feast and winter solstice.

Winter was at last unmistakable, though, the wizened burnish of autumn decimated in the forest; deep pools, mud and sodden carpets of black leaves on the dirt tracks, flocks of pigeons scavenging in the recently turned earth, the tracks of rampaging boars in his field, great wisps of vapour draping the sides of hills, drawn away by the poultice of a brief and blinding midday sun; empty cornfields, their harvested look diminishing as the stubble fell away, soaked and blackened with moisture; the grey washes of rainy skies. And the silence of the crickets; George suddenly remembered that conversation with Barbara at the beginning of their sojourn, the trill of those insects everywhere in the warm night. For how long have they been silent?

Yet all these seem to laugh, Compared with me, who am their epitaph. You had to hand it to Donne; George couldn't have expressed his own state of mind better. A bit under the belt, really, Barbara's decision to go home, he brooded. I am going to spend Christmas alone, watching my field. Oh well, one has to suffer in order that the truth may be revealed. Whatever truth it is that the powers are so penny-pinching about, sending me a piece of the jigsaw at a time, torturing me with scraps and intimations. Oh God, I need a double whiskey.

Whither, as to the bed's feet, life is shrunk. This was the thing about great poetry surely. It was there to meet you in your darkest moments, it led you by the hand through hell and out again. A light shining in the darkness, lit by someone who has been there before you, who has mapped the way in the music of the mind.

Walking in the damp cold, he came on a familiar sight: two ginger cats with human faces on the warm bonnet of a bubble car miraculously parked on a steep edge. The bubble car left barely enough room for the passage of another bubble car or one of those *Api*, the tiny three-wheeled pick-up trucks that were really only tricycles wearing overcoats.

Soon he was at the steps that led up to the big anonymous bar. He was annoyed with himself that he couldn't remember the first stanza of Donne's poem in its entirety. *'Tis the year's midnight and it is the day's... Lucy's, who scarce seven hours herself unmasks*: such beauty, how the banal perception of just another calendar day is transformed utterly... Then something about flasks that don't send out constant rays, the perfection of the rhyme. And then *The world's whole sap is sunk* and *Whither, as to the bed's feet, life is shrunk, Dead and interred. Yet all these seem to laugh, Compared with me, who am their epitaph.* Amen, how true for me this very day, as it was for Donne several centuries ago.

Those cats look human because their faces are eaten with the mange.

The bar was spacious enough. In most of the bars in the town, one game of cards at a central table, four players attended by twice as many referees, aficionados, savants of the art, players and spectators alike giving vent to frustration, opinion and triumph; with attendant gestures, the fist brought crashing down on the table to herald the winning trump that immediately after the smash falls lightly from between thumb and forefinger; the raising of victorious arms, the despair of the hand-covered forehead; this single game of cards in tandem with the television, aloft in a corner, blaring its endless production line of events at no one, was enough to ward off the devotee of the quiet drink as soon as he opened the door.

But unlike the smaller, cosier places, where card games continued all day throughout the year, even in the heat of summer, this bigger bar did not provide the atmosphere for coteries: it was not intimate enough to make a game of cards seem the most important event in the world.

The bar curved around, away from its glass-plated front to a dim back space, and George sat at a table in the dimmest corner, under the dark and mute television. There was no one else to be seen. The innkeeper was offstage, and appeared only when George called for another Vecchia Romagna, or when a fugitive figure with a briefcase came in for a quick fix of espresso, a dark stain at the bottom of a tiny cup that worked wonders of renewed alertness at flagging points of the Mediterranean working day.

By noon George had drunk a good number of brandies, and was talking to himself. A path had opened in the thicket of Italian which led him to the citadel where he kissed the sleeping beauty of proficiency, and she woke. In a twinkling, without the pain of effort or application, he had arrived at the source of it all and lovingly kissed the opening lines of Dante's *Inferno*, which had stayed in his mind from the time, thirty years before, when he had read a dual language edition of the poem:

Nel mezzo del cammin di nostra vita
Mi ritrovai per una selva oscura,
Ché la diritta via era smarrita.

And *baccio* was the word for a kiss. *Baccio alla selva oscura:* a kiss in the dark wood. *Baci Perugini* are Perugian Kisses, a very special brand of chocolates, which they sell in this very bar. I'll give her a carton of kisses for Christmas. That's it! A *cartone* of kisses in the dark wood of life, in the middle of the journey. *Cosí*, just like that. *Niente problema.*

George went once more to the counter, and this time the innkeeper was waiting for him. He had been watching George for some time, listening to him, lured out of his offstage retreat by this curiosity of a lone but talking foreigner.

He was a tall, thickset man with a life-eroded face. There was an absolute stillness about him that reminded George fleetingly of a standing stone. The innkeeper was a menhir of melancholy, a megalith with eyes. In the eyes were cloudy depths, and the world entered into those depths and was lost in there, sad that its known and secure relations had been severed and everything had drifted far apart. Each separated person and thing served its time in there trying to recover its former temporal and spatial fixity, how it had stood originally vis-à-vis the rest. George saw all this insecurity of the world in the melancholic innkeeper's face. Summoning articulacy, he dropped a few words into the well of despair.

'*É la mezzanotte del anno.* 'Tis the year's midnight and it is the day's. John Donne.'

A tiny flicker of light began to play around the innkeeper's eyes. Unaccountably, he began to shudder, at first faintly, then more perceptibly. George thought a mild earth tremor might be occurring – a weirdly localised one, confined to the other side of the counter. The innkeeper was like a stationary car whose engine had been left idling, but his face remained impassive except for the increasing flicker round the eyes.

'You keel me,' the hulk gasped finally. He leaned over the counter and gripped the outside edge to steady his spasms. 'Oh, you keel me.' His shuddering came to a halt in this bent-over position, and it seemed to George, looking down at the obliquely upturned face, that a faint smile had crossed the lips at the same moment that the light in the eyes began to fade. It was done; this tremendous exercise, in which the form of mirth and its content, light years apart, were desperately seeking one another across the expanses of space, had eventuated in a brief moment of contact. The innkeeper had committed a laugh. He had conceived a sense of humour. As a result, he rose to his full height again, a new man.

'You like Vecchia Romagna?' he asked, a new serenity resting on his weathered features. He poured George a generous measure, and then poured an equally generous one for himself. 'This drink is – how you say it in English? – on the top of the house. Merry Christmas, my friend.'

'Cheers,' said George, draining the glass. 'Salute,' said the innkeeper and drained his.

Later, at an indeterminate time in the advanced afternoon or early evening, George was retching in a toilet sink. The innkeeper was standing over him, shouting encouragement. '*Dai! Forza!* Get it from your chest, my friend. Like the old Romans, make space for more.'

George gripped the tap handles, his knuckles white. The spasms continued. He was calling Ralph on a great white telephone, and failing Ralph he called Hughey, and the innkeeper laughed hugely and clapped him on the back, then placed his hand gently on his bottom, muttering to himself *Che culo*. And laughed with the pleasure of finding a friend with a *bel culo*.

Now the spasms were the form of sickness without the content; nothing of substance remained, the running taps had drained it all away. But here, surely, was a new beginning: as the retching eased and relief oozed through George's body, there was nothing left to implicate him. He was looking into a shiny white sink, he had been given a clean slate, the jury had found him innocent, the priest in the pipes was gurgling absolution, his sins were washed away, he had cleared his debt to society, his new friend and mentor had given him the nod which was as good as a wink. Here and now, as the shades of night were falling, at an indeterminate time in the late afternoon or early evening of the winter solstice, perhaps five o'clock, it *being the shortest day*, now, here, life, drinking, began again. And poetry began again; it was the same as the relief which permeated his body. He turned from his crouched position at the sink and, standing *homo erectus*, intoned to the innkeeper the entire first stanza of Donne's poem, the previously disremembered lines snugly in place as if the retching had cleared a memory block.

'*Tis the year's midnight, and it is the day's,*
Lucy's, who scarce seven hours herself unmasks,
The sun is spent, and now his flasks
Send forth light squibs, no constant rays;
The world's whole sap is sunk:
The general balm th'hydroptic earth hath drunk,
Whither, as to the bed's-feet, life is shrunk,
Dead and interred; yet all these seem to laugh,
Compared with me, who am their epitaph.

'Bravo. Braavo!' The innkeeper clapped his large hands vigorously, joyfully. His face was suffused with an infantile joy; his life, too, had only just begun. And he loved this man who had delivered him into his new beginning just a few hours before. This miraculous obstetrician could do no wrong; if he puked into his sink, then that too was part of life's abundance. He placed his arm lovingly around George's waist and led him back to the dim-lit, empty bar.

'*Nel mezzo del cammin di nostra vita*' – he kissed George's forehead and cheeks resoundingly, whispered the great opener into his ear as a solemn confidence. He raised a didactic finger, his face stiffened into an expression importing unheard-of significance. 'In the middle of the journey of my life, I have found my Virgilio, but he does not bring me into hell, he takes me out of it. *Che strano*, how wonderful.'

The innkeeper placed George against the counter, a sack that might fall and spill its goodly contents unless attended carefully. A moment later he was looking intently at his guest from the other side, a filled glass in each hand.

'But tell me, *amico*, how is it that you can do this for me, make me see happy things, but you are not happy?'

'He saved others, himself he cannot save,' quoted George, accepting the first alcoholic drink of the rest of his life.

The party was in full swing; that is to say, insofar as a dinner party which lacked one of an expected four participants, and from which another had excused herself immediately after the meal, foregoing coffee, could be said to be in full swing. But something was swinging, nonetheless. An electricity was crackling between the two who remained.

The ceiling of the room was festooned with cheap Christmas decorations, the long table littered with plates and the remains of Barbara's carefully considered *cena*. The meal had begun with melon and prosciutto, the *primo piatto* had been tagliatelle in a salmon sauce, the *secundo* had been a goat from Rogero's freezer in the third shed, with small roast potatoes. A salad had followed, and a rather tough almond torta from a delicatessen in the town. The white wine was Orvieto and the red was Montefalco. Barbara had overcooked the tagliatelle a little, but the fish sauce was acclaimed to be delicious by a majority of two to one, the one demurrer being the cook herself, who remarked that it could have done with a touch of dill or the faintest hint of fennel. The goat, however, had warranted high praise from Rogero, not only as to the quality of the meat (which was self-praise) but also as to the *à point* nature of its cooking. Nothing could have gone wrong with the salad, given that it contained rocket from the woods and olive oil of the local cold-pressed kind. The torta: ah well, the torta were best passed over in silence, now that the coffee was good and a bottle of brandy was on the table, and two people whose proximity to one another generated a certain frisson were by chance alone together.

Mathilde had made her exit after the torta, which she had barely tasted. Her stiff departure under the pretext of having work to do was compatible with everything else about her. It was the exit of a stiff, rigor mortis on the move, a leave-taking by the categorical imperative, which loosened up the morality remaining behind. Up to now, Rogero had been as tense and stiff as Mathilde – Rogero Rigoroso, rigorously correct in everything he did and said, and on the correct side of the table, namely the opposite side from Barbara. But now Rogero the Correct Corpse felt himself loosen up in all his parts except for one part which had been uncomfortably stiff all evening from the moment he set his eyes on Barbara – dark-haired, blue-eyed, surprisingly red-lipped, her arms bare in a wine-coloured waistcoat, her lower parts poured into her striped jeans.

As Rogero's other parts loosened up, the part that had been stiff all evening remained stiff, but no longer uncomfortably so. That part had been licensed in its stiffness, and become comfortably stiffer, now that Mathilde had completed her rigorous exit, taking with her the mortifying rules and regulations that bound her and Rogero's domestic charade. The furtive eye-glances that he had been stealing all through the meal, as Barbara moved back and forth serving the various dishes, gave way to frankly lingering looks of appraisal, approval, desire, an I-like-you leer, a sustained ocular plea of come-to-bed.

When the stiffness fell from four of his five limbs, Rogero rose, taking with him to the other side of the table the limb remaining stiff, so that he and it could be close to the woman who was the cause of the current looseness and pleasant rigidity, now that the woman who had caused the uniformly uncomfortable rigidity had gone. Rogero sat right beside Barbara, poured himself a generous brandy and leered.

'What a pleasant evening. Thank you for a beautiful meal.'

'Not at all,' said Barbara. She smiled quickly at Rogero and looked away, embarrassed at his tipsy attentions, yet almost feeling vengeful enough to encourage this sudden suitor, hoping that George would walk in and find that he wasn't her only possibility in her wilderness of discontent.

Rogero groped for something to say, restraining his powerful urge to say it all by groping. With relief, he remembered a significant item from the sparse preceding conversation.

'So you're going home for Christmas? That's rather a pity. Christmas around here can be interesting, you know. The Marchesa usually has a *spaghettata* on Boxing Day. She invites all the descendants of the family's former serfs and vassals, and anyone else who lives in the valley. It's all rather a feudal hangover, but it can be quite charming.'

'Yes, I'm sure it must be.' Flattered by Rogero's oblique admission of interest, raging inwardly at George's dereliction of duty, his all-day absence, Barbara allowed herself to follow Rogero's flow a little. 'I can well imagine that spending Christmas here would be nice.'

The quick wistful glance she gave him unsettled Rogero. He sensed enormous difficulties irreconcilable with the immediacy of his need. This would normally have been enough to dampen his ardour, but Barbara somehow had a different effect on him. He plunged besottedly on, regardless of Mathilde's unhappy aura seeping from downstairs through the joins in the tiled floor, heedless of the permanent possibility of George's return.

'But look here, Barbara, if you don't mind my saying so, you make it sound as if you don't want to go. And you don't have to if you don't want to. I mean, I always thought that you two rather wanted to keep to yourselves. That is, until you invited us here tonight.'

'Well as far as I'm concerned, nothing could be further from the truth,' Barbara found herself saying somewhat heatedly, stung by the implication that she and George were of one mind on the desirability of social isolation. She thought with sudden clarity, *That drunken misfit has ruined my career break.*

'Well I don't mean any offence,' Rogero ploughed on, echoing her thoughts, 'but your friend isn't particularly gregarious. I know he's a writer and all that...'

Hurt, Barbara darted an angry look at Rogero. She controlled herself, close to tears. 'I can't stay.' She rose and began to collect dishes from the table.

Rogero silently cursed himself. The stiff part of him, the part that he liked having stiff, was suddenly flabby, and all the other parts of him, that had been flabby, began to stiffen. He poured himself a stiff drink and rigorously swallowed it. He felt it was time to go gracefully, but he couldn't bring himself to rise from the chair. Rigid, he waited for his fate to be pronounced.

Barbara put the pile of dishes in the sink, and then to his surprise, she was back in her seat, looking at him directly, talking animatedly.

'It wasn't exactly my idea to come here. And if you don't mind my saying so, *your* friend isn't particularly sociable either.'

'So that just leaves the two of us – to be doubly friendly,' Rogero said, amazed that he was saying just what he wanted to.

Barbara couldn't help laughing. 'Well, I'll give you ten out of ten for tenacity, Rogero. But let's just leave it. It's been nice to meet you informally and all that, but your friend is waiting for you downstairs, and mine is about to come home any minute, rip-roaring drunk. And tomorrow evening I'm going to London. Home to mother for Christmas.'

Rogero, loosened up again, loose now in all his parts without exception, flabby with resignation, said 'Oh well, that's life I suppose'. But having said it, he was immediately discontent about the nature of life. 'What a pity,' he sighed, and cast around desperately in his mind for some excuse to prolong the sweet agony of this woman's presence, or better again, something that would act both as a present stay of execution and also keep the future lines open. Some excuse, anything, he thought frantically, to contact her in London.

'Well, if you must go, you must,' he resigned himself foxily. 'But perhaps you can do something for me in London. That is if your social life isn't too hectic.'

'Very funny.'

'No, really, I'm not being sarcastic. I just wouldn't want to inconvenience you. You see I'm doing some research on an obscure medieval poet, and I'm told there are certain documents in the British Museum that would be useful to me. I wondered could you look these up and get me some photocopies if possible?'

'I'd be glad to.'

'You could bring them back with you,' ventured Rogero, anxious to allay a suspicion that had begun to gnaw at him. 'By the way, when are you coming back?'

'That's the problem. I really don't know. Of course I'd like to come back, sometime, but I haven't fixed a date. It's open return. George will be staying, of course,' she added with a flash of malice. 'He'll be watching the field for Christmas.'

'Watching the field?' Rogero asked, with a sinking feeling

of how dreadfully everything turns out. 'What do you mean?'

'I think it's one of yours. The one below the rise, on the other side of the house.'

'But why?'

'I haven't an earthly. I think it reminds him of his childhood.'

A pity I couldn't put some kind of metaphysical fence around it, thought Rogero. Then he might go away, and Barbara might stay. But all he said was, 'I presume Alan is going with you.'

'Yes,' Barbara said, and then, remembering how well Alan thought of Rogero, added, 'If it hadn't been for you, I'm afraid he'd have been bored to death. And thank you so much for collecting him from school today, and keeping him off my back while I was preparing dinner. He'll miss you.'

'I'll miss you both. I do hope you'll come back – soon.'

'So do I, of course. But you must give me the names of those documents or whatever you want me to look up.'

'Ah yes, of course, but that's the problem. I'll have to fax or phone the names through to you, because I haven't got them here. I need to look them up at the university.'

'I'll give you my mother's telephone number. If I'm coming back soon, I'll bring them with me. If not, I'll post them.'

'I hope it's the former,' said Rogero.

'*Che sera, sera.*' Barbara went off to get pen and paper.

Such a woman, Rogero thought, not only pretty but desirable in every way. She has poise, something indefinable, an aura.

Barbara returned and handed him a slip of paper with the London number on it. She remained standing, expecting that Rogero would now rise, say his goodbye and go. But as he looked Barbara over, for who knows maybe the last time, one part of him rose before the other parts were able. And when the other parts finally rose, they rose with the intention of bringing the part that had first risen as close as possible to Barbara, as close as she might allow. Rogero lunged at her, threw his arms around her, kissed her bare arms, sought out her lips, avidly pawed his way down her back. Barbara went dead; she didn't repulse him, simply went limp in his embrace.

'Good evening, lady and gentleman. God rest you merry. Am I interrupting something of grave import?'

George was standing in the doorway.

PART II

George woke up suddenly. A glow around the edges of the shutters signalled it was light... morning, day, afternoon, whatever. Usually early morning, because George nearly always woke prematurely, tormented out of sleep by his troubled thoughts. But this time he woke blank. Pure consciousness, without a history or a name; as it was in the beginning, consciousness waste and void. Am without an I. Blank Is-ness dumb. Being without Identity. A lens admitting no image, nothing but light.

'My God,' he said aloud, 'who am I and where am I?' He recognised the voice. It was his own, he knew now, but he still couldn't remember the name for that particular segment of reality. Then it came to him that his particular patch of existence wasn't a very happy allotment. Misery was perhaps its name, the word came to him and he spoke it. 'Misery. Pure fucking misery.' The sensation that the voice he heard came from his own mouth was reassuring, so he repeated the words over and over. 'Misery. Misery. Pure fucking misery.' An Irish accent: he must be Irish. And there was some connection, elusive, hard to pin down, between misery and being Irish. Irish Misery. Sounds like the name of a horse. 'That never won a fucking race,' he said, and laughed. Irish Mist was the name of a drink, and perhaps also of a horse... When the lemmings were finally given their freedom, they voted to do what they had always done by instinct; destroy themselves. Now that was a subtle kind of thought. Where did it come from? And where has it gone now? 'Little thoughtie woughtie, come back here,' he crooned.

By this time it had become common knowledge that his name was George. A subtle thing, like tradition; there was no identifiable exact time at which the name had been established. It was simply taken for granted now, like the fact that there was an unfinished bottle of whiskey on the locker beside the bed. From which he took a deep slug.

Silence in the room was to be expected, of course, but it was not altogether welcome. There was a touch of absence about it. On the other hand, it was good to be in control, to be the sole arbiter of what noise was to be made and when. Like now: *Lousy bitch.* Spoken slowly, lowly, with venom.

When you're not entirely in control of the sounds in a room, some of them can be unpleasant, things that you don't want to hear, such as *I couldn't sleep last night because you were snoring like a pig.* This pig image doesn't sit well with a man's self-esteem. Yes, I am free, said Sartre, but my freedom is a kind of death. Where did that come from? Same as Donne the other day, only Donne's woman hadn't walked out on him; she was carried. Not like that harridan going off and leaving me here alone, on this of all the days of the year.

Nobody had said a word about it, but it was Christmas Day. It just was. So: things are coming together. But the shape they are taking is not pleasant, and calls for more whiskey. I must have missed the Three Spirits last night, otherwise I'd be up dancing around the patio like a bi-polar depressive on the turn, telling the landlord I'd be upping his rent as a Christmas present, smearing the very walls with meat as recommended by St Francis, so that even inert matter could partake of the feast as a fit celebration of this holy and glorious day. The Franciscans are the lads for uncommon recipes: Baste well, then rub against the walls.

Christmas Day. To be spent alone, in the arsehole of rural Italy. Such a large chunk of reality to arrive in one go. Couldn't be swallowed, not without some whiskey to wash it down.

His eyes had grown accustomed to the dimness. He was sitting up in a large double bed, the sole occupant. He was sitting there surrounded by double bed, surrounded by wardrobe, chest of drawers and two small bedside cabinets, one on each side of him; surrounded by absence. On the marble top of the cabinet to his right there was a lamp; likewise on the cabinet to his left. On the cabinet to his right there was also a glass containing his false teeth, and the whiskey bottle which he now held in his hand had spent the night there, beside the false teeth. Outside the bedroom were the empty bathroom, the empty small bedroom, the empty living room. No one was out at the cooker, graciously brewing taken-for-granted coffee, being gracious about brewing coffee and about being taken for granted, in a saffron dressing gown.

And outside that again, on the third and all the other circles of hell, were Italy, Europe, the World, the Solar System, the Milky Way Galaxy, the Universe. The greatest pain was in the first circle, of course, the circle of the bedroom, the desecrated refuge of deepest intimacy. Desecration had not been alluded to until now, but although the word was unspecific, it was suddenly quite certain that there had been a desecration of considerable magnitude, and there was a lingering trace of vomit attached to the vagueness of the sacrilegious act.

Better to drag oneself out of the bedroom, at least, into the less resounding emptiness of the living room. He brought out his clothes and dressed hurriedly: subconsciously, the idea was that the more 'external' he looked, the less painful it would all be. Looking out the window as he buttoned his shirt, he had mixed feelings about the soft sunshine. On the one hand, he could walk himself to exhaustion, and outwit the suicidal theme that was already announcing itself discreetly in the jangled symphony of his desolation; on the other hand, the sweetness of the weather threatened to hone a sharper edge on his loneliness. But there was really no choice here: one last swig of whiskey and *Via!* – away with him before the devil caught up.

This was going to be one bastard of a penitential walk. For the first time, he would tackle what Barbara had called 'the Round'. He would walk down the white dirt road in the direction of town; then, at 'Wuthering Heights', a ponderously overbuilt farmhouse, half lived-in, half gap-toothedly empty, he would swing left instead of right and begin a steep, winding ascent which would bring him – eventually, if he persevered – to a ridge running along the summit of the woods and down again steeply, back to Rogero's place. Barbara (ah, Barbara!) had told him that the walk took at least two hours.

As he passed his field, now a pleasant patchwork of shades from drained green to fawn, whipped into shape by a dry wind, with shadows of violet in the tangled remnants of wild chicory, he scarcely looked at it, passed it by with only a swift sidelong glance, as a reformed narcissist might pass a mirror. He did not want anything untoward to start happening in the field. He was haunted enough as it was.

This had to be the time of fiercest determination, the beginning of the new regimen. Beginnings were always so precarious, like the beginnings of growth that one hard frost can nip. George gathered together his feelings, rounded them up; they wobbled along the road with him in the uncertain mass of a flock of sheep, kept in check by the sheepdog of his sudden fervour.

The ascending woods beside him were enveloped in a luminous ethereal haze, the faint pencil lines of denuded scrub oak scarcely discernible from the emptiness around them, with here and there a surviving garland of shrivelled bronze caught in full sunlight like a remnant of a fresco. In the flat valley on his other side, houses stood out clear, but somehow unreal, in a pastoral landscape; toy villa behind toy pines, toy olive trees, toy building-block houses. Each time George looked at it, the valley seemed more and more like a painting. He felt as if the third dimension was withdrawing, revealing itself as an illusion.

This was not pleasant. It was probably first and foremost a deceptive quality of the light, but the effect was compounded by George's general sense of unreality. And because of his drink-induced insensibility, he had felt, so far, no physical sensation associated with walking; he seemed to be floating through space muffled up in cotton wool. His feet didn't seem to make contact with the ground, or rather the feet he heard hitting the ground didn't seem to be his own. They were a law unto themselves, those feet, but somehow in their own awkward way they managed to keep up with him. This was virtual reality: road gliding along under him, wood bouncing along beside him, fields planing by. It was no way to do a penitential pilgrimage; there would have to be some effort, some discomfort.

Effort was laid on shortly after he had turned left at Wuthering Heights and began the ascent. Discomfort was quickly supplied in abundance, in the form of gasping for breath, weakness at the knees, overheating and sweat, nausea, a fainting sensation. But instead of bodily exertion distracting from mental distress, as he had hoped, on this occasion recent memory, returning in fragments, was added to his physical misery.

I'll drive them to Sant Egidio. You're obviously not in a fit condition. It was the voice of Rogero, accompanied by an image of the dapper landlord arriving around the side of the house and shepherding Barbara and Alan away from George's red Toyota towards a dark green Lancia, and coming back with a scowl to collect their cases from under George's nose.

You do not want me to fuck you and that for me is sad, and sad also for my menhir. This was the voice of Remo, the Melancholy Innkeeper, supplemented by a mental picture of a megalith standing slantwise out of the doorway of his bar. What the menhir was doing projecting from the doorway of the bar George did not have time to ponder, fighting now for strength and breath to climb the hill, fighting also the general fight against his absolute disillusionment, his betrayal by life. The point was, What can you do when you've failed and are likely to continue to fail, when your love life is totally kaput, when you're companionless against the coldness of an indifferent world? But the recent past was persistent in

presenting its random fragments.
Fuck you, George, you rotten bastard! (Barbara throws something at George. He gets sick.)
Puff, puff. Wheeze, wheeze. Rustlings on the road's margin. *What a pity you're not the one who's leaving.* (Rogero picks up the suitcases.)
Wheeze, wheeze. Puff, puff. Dart of a lizard up a rock.
Physical exertion finally got the better of mental distress only when George was certain of an imminent heart attack. He had come into a clearing in the woods, well-spaced olive trees on both sides, and a view of the valley below as he stopped and stood, coughing, heaving for air. As good a place as any to die, to breathe one's last, the flat valley bottom singing a song of everlasting tillage, the long strips of unbordered fields, the umber earth with a thin spread of new grass, the square-dug water pools, the rising smoke from here and there a chimney where the Christmas cooking had begun. He sat on a smooth-surfaced rock in the middle of the white road and, unpoetic breath whistling and straining, brain blanking, looked at the poetry of the valley in the sunlight. Already dying, taking his leave, as well he might, it was better to relax and not hold on to life; to hold on would only make the pain worse. Instead, take a last look at the centuries-old dream, at the archetype of sunlight singing in the transformed land, at the town spread out on the far slope, the crenellations of olive trees on a distant ridge repeated in the battlements of the tower, the vapours filling the spaces between the receding ranges of hills. And all the time the singing, the singing on the edge that can never be brought into clear earshot or taken to oneself, the receding nightingale, the view from the cemetery in the dream-sequence of Pasolini's *Accatone*, the music that is in but not of the air, life, the valley bottom, the saucer's rim, the centuries...

The heart attack did not occur. Instead, he got up and struggled on, every muscle in his body stretching towards some new equili-brium. That was one thing about him that the women in his life had noted, from his mother on: the iron constitution, the capacity for weathering the punishment he inflicted on himself. He had been through the stages of being afraid he was going to die, and afraid that he wasn't going to die. And now, since things hadn't got worse, they could only get better. The white road twisted upwards, flanked by olive trees and vineyards.

As George drew slowly nearer the summit of the ridge, down in the house Rogero was preparing the Christmas dinner for Mathilde and himself. It was twelve o'clock, and Mathilde had not yet risen; she was sitting up in bed taking coffee. The turkey had by now been two hours in the oven, and was doing nicely. Rogero was gathering the ingredients for the traditional pasta soup, and his thoughts were black. Mathilde always slept late on Christmas Day, as she did every Saturday, Sunday and holiday. On these days, Rogero did lunch, and brought her coffee at a quarter to twelve. She always accepted it in stony silence. Rogero accepted her stony silence as the natural order of things, on all weekends and feasts except for Christmas Day. Some vestige of Christian consciousness in him could not allow the idea that such intransigence should continue unabated on the day of Christ's birth; even in war-zones, there was a twenty-four hour truce at Christmas.

A huge log was spluttering and crackling on the open fire. A bottle of Brunello di Montalcino was breathing on the hearth. A bottle of Montefiascone white was cooling in the fridge. The dining table was laid for two: two red napkins folded into the water glasses, the smaller wineglasses beside; the Deruta plates, sideplates and soup bowls with bright blue and yellow designs, all in order, one on top of the other, flanked by items from the couple's wedding-gift cutlery. A red candle in the middle of the table was ready for lighting; an open bottle of Vecchia Romagna, from which Rogero had just poured himself a generous dollop, stood at the serving end of the table.

For Rogero, the couple's enduring marital unhappiness tended to become acute on Christmas Day, because it was the day when everything should be as it should be, and yet was so plainly not. But up to now he had managed to get through the charade every year: with the aid of a few drinks, he rode out the hours as best he could; and on Boxing Day the state of psychological warfare was normal and ordinary again, as protagonists the world over resumed their hostilities, and the news broke through with renewed malice on radio and television.

This year, however, there was a more poignant edge to his misery. He was in love with Barbara and convinced of the necessity of finally bringing things to a desperate head. If only that fool George had been the one who had left! He could have invited Barbara and Alan to Christmas dinner, and there would have been something pleasant to look forward to. Then he would have talked to Barbara, played with Alan, and Mathilde would have sat through it all, tight-lipped, eventually excused herself and retired. Barbara would have brought Alan away and put him to bed. And he, Rogero, instead of meekly closing the book on the day and staying up to watch the shapes in the embers, would have gone to Barbara's apartment on the pretext of telling her about a trip he had planned for Alan the next day, and then…

He suppressed the dawning sexual fantasy and concentrated on stirring the pot of broth. He stirred it with malicious vigour. He would like, paradoxically, to be able somehow to engineer his wife's accidental death. But 'engineer' was too strong a word for anything that Rogero was likely to do about his saturnine marriage. On the other hand, if one day he found Mathilde in a coma, he might bring himself to delay phoning the ambulance for half an hour or so…

Rogero was a very confused man. He hadn't the heart to leave Mathilde because of a mixture of guilt, pity and moral cowardice. But while, in his own self-estimation, he highlighted the pity, the reality was that he quailed before her righteous hauteur. She had the upper hand in righteousness, because of the terrible event that had blighted their marriage. Well, it hadn't seemed that bad to him at the time, but now… He suppressed the thought of it and reached for the Vecchia Romagna.

He simply couldn't bring himself to tell Mathilde, and as a result couldn't tell himself, the truth: that he not only didn't love her any more, but hated her. Therefore he fantasized all kinds of accidents happening to her, while he continued having sporadic affairs with students and junior lecturers at the university. But Barbara, he felt very strongly, was different; she was the one who could carry him through. Now he was desperate, because he had a strong suspicion that she mightn't come back to Italy. All was not well between her and George – that was certainly in his favour. And he had her London phone number, because of the inspired pretext he had concocted on the night of the dinner party. But would she ever come back, unless because of that madman, that lunatic, that *soi-disant* writer… Such a reconciliation would be life's ultimate blow.

He left the pasta soup reducing a little on the stove and looked out the window at his patio; at the bath, the bed-end, the flowerpots from which protruded only a few naked stalks. The black Aladdin's lamp dangled from its privet tree in a soft shaft of sunlight: if only there had been a genie inside it to rescue him from Mathilde! He looked beyond the trees to the soft misty straw and green tints of the field which the charlatan writer patrolled as if it belonged to him; the field that was the reason why he was going to spend Christmas hanging around the place and turning up everywhere like a bad penny.

Rogero felt a sudden hatred for the field. It belonged to him, as did most of the land and woods around the house, about seventy acres or so. But what good were fields and woods to a loveless man? He simply had to phone Barbara and tell her how he felt; otherwise his life was at an end. She was so different; she had poise, she had presence, not like the others. The thought of her maddened him, as did the awareness of the emptiness of his existence, the imminent puppet show of the Christmas dinner, the Medusa eyes of Mathilde staring at him, through him, across the table.

But he could never pluck up the courage to win a woman like Barbara. How could he, when he couldn't even find the spunk to tear himself away from his malignant emotionally threatened spouse; when he spent his life hopping from one inauthentic entanglement to the next, presenting himself to his students and young researchers as some sort of guru; name-dropping writers as if he had read the entire literature of the world, with his tactic of always pretending familiarity with an author they might mention, ah yes, Neruda, *of course*, la Rochefoucald, *indeed*, Webster, *dear me yes*, Verhaeren, *precisely*... Barbara would demand the impossible of him, simply by expecting him to be himself. She was a real person, and she would require any lover, any husband, to be real as well. No, it was without hope. What would happen if she laughed, not at his jokes, but at him? He couldn't abide that, never could; he always changed the subject if someone threatened to take what he was saying lightly or to contradict him; and he rarely laughed at anyone's jokes but his own, and was offended when people didn't see his; he even began laboriously to explain them. No, he could see neither the prospect of getting Barbara into bed by the usual techniques, nor could he become the kind of person Barbara would fall for. It was quite intolerable.

Mathilde was sitting in bed, the cup of coffee held in her upraised hand like an offering. As always on these late-rising mornings, and particularly because it was Christmas Day, she was trying to surpass herself. She was attempting to become equal to the occasion – but Christmas Day was such a big occasion! She sat there in a state of paralysis, suspended between the unforgiving person she was and the forgiving person she felt she ought to be. It really caused too much trouble to have these high standards. But it wasn't easy, either, to spend one's life in the state of not forgiving the person who shared your house. And it was worse than either of these to be between the two, hoping for some rumoured divine assistance to levitate one on to the higher plane. But an even worse prospect again was that of spending the rest of one's life alone.

If only she could take it a day at a time, forgive him just for one day, Christmas Day, and see what happened. But she was sure one couldn't just forgive a person for a day; it had to be absolute. Besides, the agony of living from day to day in a state of uncertainty as to whether the forgiveness would 'take' (like plaster to a wall or solder to a crack in metal) was the worst prospect of all. Mathilde could only live with absolutes, certainties, permanence. And although she would have preferred to be like God, and forgive absolutely and permanently, just like that, she was afraid she could never quite rise to it. On the other hand, there was a certain security in the permanence of unforgiveness; even though the attitude didn't flatter her self-image, and made her wicked in her own eyes, it was infinitely preferable to living with uncertainty from day to day or living permanently alone. The problem with living alone is that your unforgiveness can have no effect on the person not forgiven. But here, with Rogero present and guilty, and equally afraid to break away, unforgiveness conferred power, it made a dent in the way reality was ordered, it meant she was deferred to in all sorts of ways. Being propitiated was a poor substitute for being adored, true; but it meant some kind of balance against a husband's failure in true love, against his fatal indifference in a moment of crisis, against his continued unfaithfulness. At least it meant in some way that she was not to be discounted. All this would evaporate, she knew, if they separated; she would no longer be reckonable, by anyone.

Mathilde pondered all these things in her heart, as she did on many other mornings of her life with Rogero, mornings of weekends, of public holidays, previous Christmas and Easter mornings, many many mornings when she sat in bed with her mug of coffee held up like an offering and her thoughts going round and round, spiralling upwards and then back downwards, round and round, upwards again and again downwards until, like an exhausted bird, they had at last found their familiar nest, the nest of hatred, which was the only stable emotion. There was really nothing to be done about it, Christmas or no Christmas; there could be no forgiveness. As a concession to the day, however, she would talk to Rogero, but only in a businesslike way about the problem that continued to bother her...

While George was toiling up an Italian hill and Rogero, down below him, prepared dinner for his winter guest, Barbara was spending Christmas Day with her mother in a house in a London suburb.

Hilda, her mother, was a thin woman in her late sixties with a small face lined by anxiety, and eyes which alternated between sadness and quick gleams of perception. Recently conferred widowhood had made her a prey to bouts of apathy, grief and depression. In the mornings, she would wander around the house in her dressing gown looking like a witch, because she couldn't muster the energy to untangle the matted strands of her grey hair. She moved on spindly legs, looking for her glasses, forgetting that she was looking for them or finding that she already had them on, taking ages to make a cup of tea. By midday, however, she would have tied her hair up in a bun and dressed herself. After that she became more energetic, more determined to keep house and keep up appearances; and now that Barbara was back home, now that she had flesh and blood for company, her own flesh and blood, along with this midday release of energy came talk, a monologue of curiosity, speculation, questions.

'Something's seriously amiss, my dear, isn't it? Why don't you tell me? Why hasn't that George fellow come back with you?'

Hilda had never really approved of George, partly because he was Irish, partly because she saw him as a waster, a broody ineffectual sort, a predator who was sponging on her daughter's income, as if there hadn't been enough demands on it already because of Alan's needs. And what with Alan's father's being another waster, although this time, it had to be said, an English one, and Barbara's getting nothing from him either because of the lack of a settlement, the whole business was really a disaster in Hilda's eyes, but just the kind of disaster that Barbara was prone to get herself into. In this, she was just like her father, who had all his life been a prey to his sympathy for self-styled victims of society, spongers really, who of course never repaid him, so that she, Hilda, had been left with little more than the house and the widow's pension when he died.

'Really, Barbara, I had such serious misgivings. I'm so glad to see you and Alan back again. Honestly – to take unpaid leave of absence and go off to a country where no one speaks English, frittering away your savings. And with George, who is practically penniless, and seems quite unemployable at this stage.'

'Mum, how often have I told you that George came into a small legacy on the death of an uncle? He's not penniless. It was not only my savings that supported us. George was at least paying his way, whatever else you say about him.'

'Ah, but what will happen when he has spent his legacy? I bet he hasn't done a thing to earn any money, has he? You remember he told me he could easily get a job teaching English? Did he even try to get one? I daresay not. In any case, I don't think those Europeans are really interested in learning English...'

Barbara had parried her mother as best she could for her first couple of days back home, and managed to keep her own counsel. But this was Christmas Day, this was the Christmas Dinner; in front of her was a cooked turkey which she prodded uncertainly with a carving knife, unsure about carving because for the whole of her previous life there had been a man who did it, either her father, who was dead, or George or her husband, who were as good as dead. Here were two women without men, mother and daughter, in the dining room of her childhood, its walnut table covered now with the lacework tablecloth she had brought from Italy, her mother's Christmas present bought on the day of her blood test... and the result of that blood test still pending because of another bureaucratic cockup! And there was Alan, a boy without a father, quiet, gone into himself because of all that had happened; without appetite, fidgeting with a Christmas cracker. Two manless women, a fatherless boy, shadows of absences falling with winter light on glass and crockery, a mother getting on her daughter's nerves, still probing now as Barbara's hand faltered on the carving knife that refused to slice the celebratory turkey because there was nothing to celebrate. And irony of ironies, the tablecloth was Irish lace; although it was made on an island in Lake Trasimene, an Irish nun had brought the technique there at the end of the nineteenth century.

Barbara steeled herself, and the turkey grudgingly yielded a few thin slices of its breast.

But after dinner, while Alan played with a remotely controlled toy car, and she and Hilda had gone to the front room to avoid the din, Barbara knew that the charade could continue no longer. Initially she had considered phoning one of her school colleagues, a woman who had been a confidante, but her pride had prevented her. She had left the school with a flamboyant farewell party, in the aura of her fellow teachers' admiring envy: here was a Miss Butterpat who wasn't content to fill her head with fantasies of adventure, but took the necessary steps to realize them. However, Barbara couldn't trust her confidante not to spread the news among her colleagues, and couldn't endure the thought of their suppressed glee at the shame of her crestfallen return, in need of a shoulder to cry on, the great artistic escapade in a shambles less than halfway through the supposed year of liberation. But now, in the late afternoon of a Christmas Day full of absences and shadows, she felt that she must speak to someone, anyone, even her mother.

Soft sunlight, cool breeze, the fibres of George's bodily being stretched to their utmost, bones creaking in pilgrimage behind the impatient spirit, the persistence of memory.

It was now firmly established that Remo had propositioned George on Christmas Eve. He had closed his bar early to be alone with him, expelling the customers to their great annoyance. Remo had been hot and bothered all evening as George drank, oblivious of his padrone's passion. Suddenly, when the doors of the bar were shut, it had all been revealed, the hugely inflated menhir of the large Etruscan had come out to explain its owner's hasty and precipitate actions. *It love you too, like me.* And George, shocked into brief sobriety, had made for the door, and Remo had come after him, begging him to stay. A tussle had followed, and George made his escape, looking back once to see the Etruscan, his monument unveiled, standing melancholy in the doorway. Following fast on the intemperate expulsion of his clients, this act of exposure was surely the end of his business if it had been seen by anyone in the town. Oh my God, George fretted; it didn't happen, did it? But if it didn't, how can these lurid images swim into my mind?

Another summit showing up there ahead, the sky pouring through behind the road's visible limit, no longer a summit as George approached it, the road twisting upwards again, another house raising its head, lifting out of the ground. When George was a child, he loved these illusory summits, never knowing whether the world would come to an end at the next, with a drop into the void; the line between road and sky was at least the edge of a cliff, it had to be. Walking the boreens of his townland with his mother and brothers, he had played a game of betting on the next horizon; and surely he must win sometime, because the world had to come to an end, it couldn't go on forever.

'And then, one day, the world did come to an end. You were still a child, but your childhood came to an end.'

This was a voice speaking inside his head, but the content it expressed didn't seem to be his own, because he didn't know what it meant. The voice put paid to his game of road-watching, and he looked up apprehensively. There was a house beside him on the right, a house of green grilled shutters, the paint patched and peeled, the walls of mortared stone repaired in segments with garish red brick. The wind was stronger at this more exposed height, and a few loose shutters moved and creaked, revealing the glassless window frames of another deserted dwelling. A tinkling was carried on the wind.

Just beyond this house, the road divided; the first track

ran along the flat edge towards another house, the second track rose through an olive grove towards another summit. Among the olive trees, sheep grazed, the bells around their necks creating a continuous lightfooted stampede of tinny jangling that darkened and brightened like the scene itself. The olive terraces had mouldered back into the landscape, leaving their traces in an unevenness of humps and hillocks. This was the road George took, ever ascending, ascending now among hideous ancient boles, split and deformed, eaten away and hollowed out, twin trunks locked in an appalling copulation.

The sheep moved away down the slope, tinkling, taking with them their timeless image of pastoral tranquillity, leaving George to contemplate the ugly faces of the damned imprisoned in the olive trees, no longer soft sensual greedy flesh but hard impermeable wood. They looked out at him, venomously and yet beseechingly, as he passed. One of them was a face he thought he should know, but they kept changing into one another.

'You never saw the faces of the others,' said the voice in his head. Then he remembered a line of Hamlet's: *Oh my prophetic soul, my uncle!*

He belched a huge belch with an aftertaste of whiskey and a slight taste of sick. He was standing in the middle of the olive grove, Dante after a rough night, having lost his guide, not sure what circle he was in, only certain that this was Hell. He struggled on towards the gap at the top of the grove.

At first Hilda wasn't very responsive to Barbara's story. She was disappointed to find her suspicions confirmed: her daughter was home only because things hadn't gone well. She clamped her lips on the 'I told you so' they wanted to utter and listened silently, nursing a grim, almost vengeful satisfaction in the knowledge that she had been right about George all along.

'It was all a bit unreal,' Barbara was saying. 'At first it was unreal like a beautiful dream, so I didn't question it. I basked in the sun and waited for things to start happening. Renewed love life – you know, Mum – and happy family scenarios in a pastoral setting, trips to Rome and Florence and looking at all that wonderful art. I didn't really take in the discordant note that was always there, on the edge of the music. There was all this painting I had the opportunity to do at last, and I swept the discordant bits under the carpet – I mean the haggling about whose turn it was to take Alan for the day or collect him from school, the standoffishness of the landlord and landlady, the language barrier. I ignored them because every morning there was no stifling job to go to, just more sun and more perceptions. But there was George, retentive as ever, not measuring up to the challenge, in fact slowly going to pieces as it turned out. He had decided to take a year off writing, and the result seems to have been that he projected his imagination on to reality. It must have been something like that. But in the end he wasn't there for me at all, except as a flaw in the background, something menacing in the corner of my eye...'

Hilda thought, How typical of our Ba-ba, out there with that madman and not to notice the danger, putting the best possible construction on everything. Just like her poor father.

'The weather was always mild and sunny in the late morning and early afternoon, give or take a day, right into November and December. You could sit out a lot of the time. The dogs would suddenly howl, even in broad daylight, for no apparent reason. I'd take my easel and palette and go up the lanes. I'd find a good viewing point and start painting. So peaceful, sheep with tinkling bells, then absolute silence. When I painted, I sort of opened out. I became one with the landscape. At times it was ecstatic, but inwardly I was hatching a nightmare.'

'And soon enough, strange things began to happen to me

too, and to my pictures. There were three dogs on the farm and we used to take them with us on walks. Well, Alan and I used to. George never took a decent walk, almost from the start he abandoned the physical fitness aspect of our year. Anyway, I'd bring my sketch pad on these long walks and when we took a rest halfway, on the steps of a deserted house, I'd sketch the dogs. But I began to see all kinds of sinister things in the faces of the dogs, one in particular. And curiously enough, his name was Giorgio... You know, Mum, the Italian for George.'

Hilda couldn't make much of what Barbara was now saying, couldn't understand that kind of arty talk or psychoanalytic introspective stuff. But she understood well enough that her daughter had been taken in once more, by another ne'er-do-well. Her maternal feelings burgeoned under the ash of widowhood, like eucalyptus after a forest fire. She formed a fierce resolution to put her daughter's feet firmly on the ground again. But first, for the sake of her own lingering curiosity, she demanded to know how it all ended.

'What happened, basically, was I gave George an ultimatum. Either get back on track with our agreed plan for the year – which involved him doing his share of the everyday tasks and being generally responsive – or else I was leaving. But it didn't work, Mum. In fact George got worse. I had to confront my fear of doing pictures of they. There was a good opportunity to do it when the dogs were taken away for a while because someone was laying poison around the forest. I don't think I'd have managed to draw them from life.

'So I went off and left George to take care of the housework. I'd go each morning to a quiet place far away from the farm, and draw the dogs in their absence. But when I'd come back in the evening, the dishes were still beside the sink, only one or two of them washed, Alan's bed still undressed. George had done nothing except have a vision or hear voices. It all came to a head when I arranged a dinner party for the landlord and landlady.

George went to town in the morning to get me some fennel, and didn't return. The landlord had become quite friendly by that time, and he actually brought Alan home from school in the afternoon, because George had gone with the car and completely forgot about collecting him.

'At the end of the dinner party, Rogero – the landlord – became more friendly than was proper as soon as his wife had excused herself. And George arrived home bang at the strategic moment when he tried to grope me. I had nothing to do with it, Mum. Don't look at me like that.'

'Go on,' said Hilda.

'George was out of his senses. He staggered to the bathroom after a slurred sarcastic comment, and Rogero left immediately with profuse apologies. I expected George to come back at me, I was steeling myself for a ferocious row, when I heard him getting sick. After that, silence: he must have fainted. A long time passed. I got a bit worried and went in. And there he was, stretched on the floor. There was a box of Perugino chocolates, sprayed with vomit, lying beside him. He was snoring like a pig.

'That was the end, Mum. That box of chocolates was intended for me. And if he hadn't been such a pig, you know, it might almost have worked – because I told him a few weeks before that I really liked them and it was one thing he'd remembered. But seeing them covered with vomit struck me as just about right. The chocolates were like his affection for me, what was left of it, and he had puked all over them. It was like a sign. Are you all right, Mum?'

Hilda had her hand to her mouth. 'Could you spare me those details, dear?'

'I'm sorry. Can I get you a glass of water?'

'I think I need a little air.'

'Shall we have a little walk, just up and down the street a bit? I'll tell Alan. We won't go very far.'

'All right, dear. I think it would be best for me.'

The two women put on their overcoats and hats and walked out, Barbara linking her mother by the arm, careful to walk slowly. The afternoon was cold but fine, the light was grey and fading. There was no one to be seen, and only the very occasional sound of a car from the high street. The side street where Hilda lived was narrow, curved and quaint, with old-fashioned street lanterns, and a very curious moulding above the lintel of every house: the face of an old man, hard to know whether he was grinning or grimacing, wearing a nightcap that looked like a bandage unravelling. Whenever Barbara looked at one of these mouldings, it reminded her of Marley's face on Scrooge's doorknocker.

They walked a bit up the street. Barbara caught a glimpse through one of the windows of a number of people around a table wearing paper crowns, but there was no light in many of the windows. These dwellings were gradually being taken over as town houses by business and media people who had more substantial homes elsewhere. Hilda was one of the last of the old residents.

'I feel much better,' Hilda finally announced. 'Let's go back now. Continue with your story, but pass over the disgusting bits.'

'Well, there's not much left to tell. I was leaving in any case the next day, but I decided to go earlier than necessary. As soon as I got up, I packed our bags, woke Alan, went down to Rogero's apartment to ask him for a taxi number. Rogero volunteered to take us to the airport himself. He was only too glad to help, I suppose, to make amends for his indiscretion. But while we were waiting for him to freshen up, out comes George, who had been sleeping on the fouton. *Why are you leaving so early?* he demands. *You ought to know*, I said. *Just tell me one thing*, he goes on, *why did you throw the chocolates I bought you into the bin?* It was so quaint, it might have been amusing if this had been just another tiff. I would have expected him to ask what was going on between me and Rogero. And then I said something terrible to him which I won't repeat here. I said it with such venom it stopped him in his tracks. Luckily, Rogero arrived at that point and rescued us. That's about it, Mum. Here I am.'

'How awful for you my poor Ba-Ba.' Hilda's arm tightened on Barbara's. 'And how awful for Alan.'

The lantern lights on the street were just beginning to glow. The pair were almost back at the house.

'Well, it wasn't all that awful for me, Mum. In a way it was like waking up after a bad dream. Except that the rotter has screwed up my plans. But Alan is taking it rather badly.'

'Tell me about this Rogero person. Didn't you say that he used to take Alan with him round the farm and that sort of thing?'

'Yes. And Alan misses him. Rogero was very good with him, and very kind. I also feel that he became very attached to Alan. He and his wife are apparently childless.'

'Well, it's really out of the question, my dear.' Hilda was at the door, about to insert the key. She turned and eyed Barbara sternly. 'Not that you have any soft spot for Rogero, of course.'

'Certainly not,' Barbara countered sharply. 'He's so boringly pretentious. He's a name-dropper, he idolizes the local aristocracy. He despises George only because he expected to have a successful writer as a tenant, so that he'd have another name to drop, and then he must have discovered on the grapevine that George wasn't very highly regarded. All I'm saying is that he has been good to Alan. And I suppose,' she added wistfully, 'I've always thought that he's unhappy, and that's why he's so pretentious. He's just built this façade around himself to hide the emptiness.'

They stood facing one another in front of the door, Hilda's key-holding hand waving like a metronome at high speed.

'Don't even think about it. It's out of the question. You must face up to reality, Barbara. One broken marriage, unresolved, one catastrophe with a waster, a failed writer, and then to go and break up someone else's marriage, all for a man who is really a sort of... a sort of mirage to a thirsty traveller.'

The door opened from the inside. Alan was there, his face beaming.

'Mum, I've just been talking to Rogero. He called to wish us all a happy Christmas. He has a present for me. I said I'd go and get you, but he was in a hurry.'

Hilda's eyes fixed accusingly on Barbara.

'But I never...' Barbara was stuck for words, not quite sure what it was that she never.

'You need to rein yourself in, my dear, and that's the end of it.'

'Oh Mum!'

'When are we going back to Italy?' asked Alan.

When George passed through the gap at the top of demented olive grove, he was on the true summit of the hill. A breathtaking view opened out before him; beyond the rolling hills, the snow-capped Appenines, the spine of Italy that stretched all the way from the plain of the Po to Calabria, rose up in peaks and double peaks and massive wrinkled hides, retreating away towards the south, like a great ragged flotilla of icebergs, a march of defeated giants.

George's spirit lifted at the sight. His body was also relieved to see that the road now ran bumpily along the level. He was on a ridge of new promise. As he stood for a few minutes to admire the *vista panoramica*, his mind and heart expanded at the expanse of it all, his laboured breathing began to even out into a deeper rhythm of newfound resources. Little waves of achievement and delight passed through all those rudely awakened muscles that had complained bitterly at first, but were now glad to be of some use again, to exercise their power once more. George's secret thought was that if he could climb the hill in this mental and physical condition, and on Christmas Day at that, a day traditionally devoted to torpor, then everything was possible: longevity, post-meridian sex, the return of sanity; with longevity and sanity the possibility of long-postponed fame; with sex renewed inspiration; with physical fitness and a commonsensical regimen, reconciliation with Barbara. This was not a Christmas for nostalgia, no more than it would be a New Year of futile waiting for the lucky break, the sudden stroke of good fortune, the long-expected unexpected letter. This was a time for shaping the modest life within his reach into a tolerable prospect of middle and old age.

The road hugged the edge of a steep, thickly covered slope, a hanging forest of scrub oak reaching out of an ivy undergrowth. Ivy also draped some of the thin boles, lichen brightened here and there on the branches, green and mustard in beams of chapel-quiet sunlight. George kept an eye out for a break in this density, through which he might be able to look down at the house and field. He seemed to remember that Barbara had told him there was such a coin of vantage on the summit. Ah, Barbara! The wood fell away between the dense interpeeping trunks into depths of ivy, lichen and silence. He drew back from their invitation and moved on.

His mood had changed: too much darkness between the trees. Darkness, and demonic creatures darting from one shadow to another, watching him. They were the thought-police; they were watching his thoughts, they could see into his head. He quickened his pace; he had to find the Barbara-place where he could look right down to the level, to the outposts of civilization that clung to the valley.

At last he came over a small road horizon to an expanse where the scrub oak had been thinned considerably; tall gangly sentinels with high scant heads stood about eight to nine meters apart in this clearing that descended the entire slope, down the land's tumbled tiers, its leaps and bounds. And there at the bottom was the house; he immediately recognised the slant of the white wall that bannistered the steps to his balcony, he recognised the long rectangular shape of the general mass, its changes of colour as a plastered and whitewashed wall gave way to one of mortared stones. He even picked out a faint blur of red by the balcony steps that must have been his Toyota. And there, a little to the left, triangular, with one slightly curved side where the white road ran, was his field.

'I have been asked to show you something,' said a mellifluous voice.

George looked around. There was no one there. He was standing near a tall scrub oak whose leaves had all fallen away on one side of the trunk but were intact on the other. It struck him immediately that the tree looked like a tall gaunt angel in profile, something from a fresco-painter with a penchant for delicately elongated figures. As he examined it, the gangly tree seemed to wrap itself in a mist or flowing luminous garments. The picture blurred and cleared, blurred and cleared, like television on the blink. A head with flowing hair; an arm with flowing sleeve, gesturing in the direction of the field. No, it's only a tree, he decided, leaves rustling in the breeze, a tree that looks like a bloody angel. He had supped long enough with hallucinations to be unduly bothered. He turned to resume his survey of the house and field.

'The angels of the middle realm have sent me,' continued the voice. Its mellifluous tone struggled to rise out of the gravitational pull of a harsher sound, somewhere between the rustling of withered leaves and the creaking of wood. 'They have asked me to show you what they know. For your salvation.'

'Fuck my salvation,' George roared, out of patience with the persistence of the hallucination. *And fuck you too, whoever or whatever you are–* he wanted to say that, too, but found he couldn't speak. And when he tried to walk on, he found that he couldn't move.

'You will not be able to speak or move any part of you but the eyes until these revelations are complete,' continued the voice. 'Your eyes, however, will be granted complete freedom in relation to the spectacle, with zoom and X-ray facilities. You will continue to look down at the arena of your contest with despair. The entire pantomime, brought to you courtesy of the angels of the middle realm, for the salvation of your soul, will take a mere ten minutes of your mortal time. Then you will be free to go and choose the righteous path. In the evening of life they will examine you on love. Terms and conditions apply.'

The scene down in the valley dimmed to darkness. George's eyes were fixed on the field. He could make out, under an ersatz moonlight, three figures digging a hole, taking turns. They shovelled swiftly, frantically. At a distance was a strange contraption like a space satellite. George willed his eyes to zoom in on the space satellite, and saw that it was a cement mixer.

He began to discern headstones, crosses, and the shape of a truck. There were other human figures, too: they stood at a remove, looking elsewhere; watchers for trouble.

The men's digging slowed. Two of them laid aside their shovels and watched the third as he scraped a last few shovelfuls of clay out of the grave. George saw that the grave already contained a coffin. There was a dull sheen of brass. He zoomed in further, and saw the name on the brass plate of the coffin: there was an ecclesiastical title – Very Rev Canon – and then the name of his priest uncle (the surname was George's own) followed by RIP.

By this time, all of the figures below, diggers and watchers, had come together to wheel the cement mixer nearer the hole, over the uneven ground. Some pulled it, some pushed it, some cursed it, some shushed the cursers up; slowly it approached the mouth of the grave. There seemed to be many more figures than there had been, all hell-bent on pouring cement over his uncle's coffin. Was this being done to make sure that he never rose again – or to prevent the desecration of his remains?

Unbearably curious, George willed his vision to penetrate the brass and wood of the coffin. Another shock: he saw a face in grim repose that looked like that of his new friend, the innkeeper. This is a bad dream, he thought; if only I could muster the strength to wake up. He continued to stare at the face, at the same time making an effort of will to regain wakefulness. What he now saw were blackened, burnt features that didn't look like anybody's face at all. But a face soon returned out of the embers: this was indeed the face of his uncle, which bore a passing resemblance to his new friend's only in the length of its bent-boned nose. The expression on the face, however, was far from the kindly melancholy of the innkeeper.

The field-watcher now saw his uncle's eyes opening, glowing with the ardour of damnation, watching him watching. The mouth formed a hideous grin and spoke in an uneven staccato like the crackling and splitting of wood in a fire: *I ruined you, and you…are rebegot…of absence, darkness… death…*

The words jumbled and spat against one another as the graveyard scene disappeared in smoke and flames. And still George was not able to move.

The voice behind him said, 'You are retrievable – just about. There is a little more you need to know, but I must leave. Remember to thank the angels of the middle realm for their interest in your development. Prayers may be recorded for quality control and training purposes. Now you will watch the house.'

George watched the house; he didn't have any choice. Two glowing lumps, like embers, came out of the landlord's apartment. They became figures of a thin man and a plump woman who stood under the balcony and waved their arms at one another. The thin man struck the plump woman and she fell to the ground. He stood there with arms akimbo, watching as she got to her feet. She went back into the house, came out carrying an urn-like vessel, and showed it to the man in a gesture of supplication. He turned his back. Going down on her knees, she raised the urn towards the sky. She began to wail uncontrollably, hugging the vessel to her breast. A ghostly white van appeared driving into the forecourt; three skeletal figures got out and bundled the plump woman into the back of the van. They tried to wrest the urn from her grasp but she clung to it, screaming. The three skeletons conferred briefly with the thin man, who shrugged, then two of them got into the back of the van beside the woman. The thin man stood watching as the other skeleton got in the front and drove away.

    The thin man remained waiting under the balcony. A light appeared in the wood beyond the animals' compound, going round in circles but gradually making its way back towards the house. The light became a svelte female figure with easel and shopping bag, coming down the road. She went over to meet the thin man and talked to him for a long time. They went up the steps. On the balcony of George's apartment, they embraced passionately. Shortly a leaf-green flame appeared on the balcony beside them, became a boy, and the three figures held one another and danced around, transmuting as they danced into one golden flame with leaf-green edges.

    Now the field began to move and seethe and bubble and form a vortex like a whirlpool, which spread to the edge of the bluff where the house stood. Suddenly the vortex belched a huge flame that leaped into the sky. Hot embers covered the surrounding countryside and dropped on the house, which caught fire. The golden flame on the balcony changed into three figures fleeing up the road, escaping.

George found that he was lying on the dusty path. Above him, a tall scrub oak rattled its ragged leaves in the wind. He stood up slowly, brushed the dust from his clothes, and walked on. He began to sob uncontrollably.

Down in the house, the Christmas Dinner was in full swing, in silence. In the middle of the table, the thick red candle had burnt out a hollow around its wick and the flame now seemed to be floating in a pool of candlefat. Mathilde and Rogero sat opposite one another. Mathilde stared straight through Rogero's head as if it had been transparent; she looked out through the window of his head at some distant glacial Alpine peak. She munched imperceptibly, mouth politely closed, on a piece of turkey breast. Every quarter of an hour she would take a tiny sip of wine and wipe her mouth with her napkin.

At the end of the long narrow room, beneath the big brass hood of the fireplace, the underside of the yule-log was being eaten away by its own hot ash. An occasional billow of smoke sent Rogero scurrying to adjust the damper. He was attentive to maintaining every aspect of exterior propriety.

The traditional pasta soup, though it had reduced a little too much, had been quite presentable. The turkey, which had been doing very nicely all along, was very nicely done in the end; the breast was moist enough without being too moist. Mathilde hadn't much of an appetite, but if there had been someone with an appetite inside that cold statuesque female form from which Rogero continually averted his eyes, she would have found the breast tender and succulent, quite to her liking. Rogero, on the other hand, favoured the leg. He was a leg man rather than a breast man, if it came to the crunch, though he was also partial to a bit of breast. This time, he sufficed with half a leg and no breast, because the turkey had very large legs.

The observances required that he remain capable of walking a straight line until Mathilde 'retired', so he presented as a leg man, but not yet footless, who sat with his back to the window; a leg man not yet footless but drinking at a much faster rate than his wife; a transparent leg man who, coupled with the window, served as double glazing through which his frozen spouse looked out at an invisible sister Alp. Mathilde was a snow-woman looking out through a window-man who was still steady, not yet footless but almost legless as mouthfuls of turkey disappeared below the frame of a Swiss vista.

There's something in this notion of aura, Rogero thought, as he sat with his back to the window, and poured himself another glass of Brunello di Montalcino, an act which required a summoning of courage under the unremitting stare of Mathilde. There's something about her presence that reduces me to a pasta soup inside. Something I can't penetrate. Something hypnotic about her that makes me stay here eating with her and attending to her, building up the observances for her as if she were some baleful deity. Something that wards off communication, something in the air around her that jams my transmitter. Pretty soon it'll come to it that I can't say a word to her, never mind tell her to get the hell out of my life.

The plum pudding was being heated on the cooker in the kitchen recess; its thick silverfoil casing knocked against the side of the pot of boiling water in which it had been half-immersed, a continuous thum bubble bubble thum bubble thum bubble, steam now on one side of the room as well as smoke on the other. The plum pudding was an annual gift from Ireland which Rogero appreciated, since he couldn't stomach the dry-as-dust panettone which Italians ate at Christmas. He liked plum pudding very much, both as a gustatory experience and in its potential for drawing out the day's ritual. From the taste side of things, or the gourmet point of view, there was really nothing nicer than plum pudding; a pity that eating it in front of Mathilde tended to spoil his appetite, twinge his stomach a bit, as if every mouthful chalked him up higher on her mind's graded scale of gluttony. From the ritual aspect, however, the plum pudding was a welcome prolongation of ceremony: the idea was to extend the liturgy till Mathilde's early bedtime, thereby avoiding an uncomfortable period in which she might raise thorny questions.

Rogero rose and cleared the used plates and cutlery. He turned off the cooker, took the pudding out of the water with oven gloves, tipped it out of its casing on to a plate, carried it reverently to the table, doused it with Courvoisier in the absence of Hennessy, stuck a sprig of privet into its flat top in the absence of holly, and set it alight. He stood back to admire. The flames slithered blue and gold around its dark brown surface, as if they couldn't find a grip, and fell off into nothingness. Rogero summoned a sense of occasion from the recalcitrant depths of his soul; this was the moment for seasonal greetings.

'Merry Christmas,' he said to no one in particular, avoiding Mathilde's eyes. He could have been saying it to the pudding. He waited for the return greeting to tumble out of her mouth like two lumps of ice on to the table, but all Mathilde did was raise her hands in a gesture of refusal; no pudding for her. Rogero cut a single portion, placed it in a bowl and sat down to eat it, crouching under Mathilde's gaze as if by bending low he could avoid the indigestion of her watching. Then, unexpectedly, Mathilde spoke, and Rogero almost choked on his first mouthful.

'When you have finished eating, Roger, I would like to speak with you.'

Rogero took a long drink of water, staring at her as he drank. With an effort he tore himself away from the twin sarcophagi of her eyes and poured himself a large measure of brandy. 'Cheers,' he said with reckless inappropriateness, and knocked it back.

'And I'd like to be able to speak to you, Roger, before you have had any more to drink, if you don't mind.'

'But of course, Mathilde, of course,' said Rogero as the courage of the brandy suffused his head. 'We have much to talk about.'

'What I have in mind will not take long,' said Mathilde with the finality of Alpine mountain tops, 'and afterwards, I shall retire to my room for the evening. I have no wish to discuss anything with you other than a matter I brought up a number of weeks ago, about which you have done nothing. You know what I mean, I'm sure, or rather *whom* I mean.'

The indirect reference to George had a curious effect on Rogero, acting as a charm to break the spell of ritual and pathological avoidance. It came as a giant shadow cast by a dawning future of tormented love and vicious jealousy. It was the shadow of the Guardian of the Narrow Pass, whom he must fight to win his escape from a remaining lifespan of perfect emptiness. The allusion to George dropped into the topsoil of Rogero's mind like a dragon's tooth, out of which instantly sprung a hugely inflated armed warrior. And suddenly George was everywhere: the Man on the Hill was a pantheistic presence in the house, filling it; the forever hoverer, the Hic et Ubique, was now the tallow and the wick, the pool of grease, the flame's Duchy of Light and its Papal State of Dark, the plates and their ancient design, the empty wine bottle that begged another, the condensation on the wall of the kitchen recess, the fire, the ash, the smoke's acridity and the half-eaten log, the hood, the damper, the hearth, the poker, the turkey still intact and the turkey in the gut, the pudding with its neatly segmented cleft, the churning in the stomach, the man window and the glass window, the gazer, the gazed through and the gazed upon, the glacier snug on its alp, the field in which had grown overnight an Enormous Turnip which they tried and they tried and they tried but could not pull up.

'I don't want to discuss it,' said Rogero with restrained fury and incipient incoherence.

'I beg your pardon? This is not a question of your wanting to discuss it. It is incumbent on you to discuss it, and *do something about it*. The fact is, I have been borne out in my apprehensions. That man is presently living here *alone*, having driven out his consort and her offspring by his appalling behaviour. He is now more dangerous than ever, with no restraining influences, and you don't want to discuss it. Look at me, Roger.'

Rogero glared at her, riled out of reason by the words *consort* and *offspring*. 'I said I don't want to discuss it. I won't discuss it, not on Christmas Day. Nor, for that matter, any other day.'

Mathilde rose. 'Very well, Roger. I see that I have left my reasonable request too late. You're obviously in your cups earlier than usual. I shall go straight to my room. Please oblige and turn up the heating a little.'

'By all means, my dear. But we must be careful we don't *melt*, mustn't we?'

'I'll thank you to refrain from such remarks. Why don't you phone one of your many women friends and spend the rest of the day with her? I'm sure you'd be more congenial to one another.'

'Mustn't turn up the heating too much. We must be careful the glacier doesn't become an iceberg and melt away into nothing, mustn't we?'

Mathilde went straight to her room without replying. Rogero, worked up into a rage, followed her down the passageway and stood shouting at her door.

'But of course you must retire, my dear, mustn't you? You haven't really advanced for twenty years, have you? When was the last time you made an advance? You made enough of them twenty years ago to last me a lifetime in hell, didn't you? Why don't you retire good and proper, once and for all, out of my life? Tell you what, I'll pension you off and you can retire to one of those log cabin hotels in Switzerland, up among your glacial first cousins. But we better not turn up the heating too much here oh dear no. Otherwise, we'll have a flood on our hands.'

Mathilde stood on the far side of the room, the lugubrious meaningless double bed between her and Rogero, the bed they had once slept in together and made love in, little kitsch panels of repoussé work adorning the top of the high bedstead, meaningless little naked bodies among clusters of grapes. Her eyes filled up and two tears rolled down her cheeks. With a final effort, she held her terrible dignity long enough to say 'Please leave me, Roger' and see him turn his back and go. Then she collapsed on the bed, sobbing loudly.

Rogero, passion spent, damage done, sat by the fireside, having first made sure to pour himself a generous glass of Courvoisier. He watched a small black scorpion advance towards the heat and then retire, going round and round, advancing and retiring. Life's movement, advance and retire. Advance to the top of the hill, and retire down the other side. Over the top. Barbara was his last chance before he went over the top for good. He mustn't throw his hat at her.

It was getting dark outside. On one side of him the log glowed and on the other, on the table, the candle flame flailed about, nearing its end. He could hear Mathilde's sobbing in the distance, some inconsolable creature crying in the centre of the great maze of its underground burrow. Laying it on with a trowel, he thought; making a meal of it as usual. He felt vaguely ashamed.

Usually, after a row like this, he would go and apologize to Mathilde in a while. And she would cry in his arms and he would say *There now, there now.* And Mathilde would say something like *Oh Roger, who'd have thought it would have turned out like this? Haven't we suffered enough?* And he would know what she meant but not want to talk about it, so he'd say

It'll be all right, my dear; you'll see. And he'd tuck her into bed, with her hot water bottle if it was winter. Then the whole cycle would start all over again, newly invigorated with some kind of human warmth for a spell…

He heard footsteps and a familiar huffing and puffing in the silence. He looked up and saw the shadowy figure passing the window; it was the Man on the Hill in the flesh, returned, rounding the house, ascending the steps to his lonely apartment. He heard the footsteps overhead, pacing; then the muffled blare of television. He jumped out of his chair, went to his room and got the slip of paper on which Barbara had written her phone number.

On Christmas night, George dreamt that he was at the post office, searching dementedly in his pigeon hole for mail. He finally extracted a postcard – a difficult operation, as the card had many strings attached to it, a spaghetti of strong elastic bands that pulled against him. He knew that if he didn't hold on to the card with all his strength, it would shoot back into the pigeon hole forever.

Entangled in elastic, slammed up against the wall of letter boxes, he managed, after much struggle, frustration and interruption, to read the postcard. It was from the dogs in the south of the province, and said: *Saluti from Babs Giorgio and Carinosa. We are aware of your unfortunate condition. You are in grave danger. We are coming home to protect you. Then you must take us for Walkies. WALKIES IMPORTANT NNB. The hermit good lives in the wood. Arrivederci.*

PART III

On St Stephen's Day, George woke to the barking of dogs. His body was sore and stiff, but he hauled himself to the living room window and looked out. A white car was parked beside his red Toyota, one he had not seen before – an Alfa Romeo saloon with a covered trailer. And sure enough, there were the three dogs, bounding up and down the forecourt, pausing to sniff at familiar shrubs and herbs: delighted to be back in the old place. Babs looked up at George's window and seemed to wink, and suddenly the three dogs bounded off in the direction of his balcony steps. In a moment they were outside the apartment door, circling the balcony, pawing the glass.

George remembered his dream of the previous night: WALKIES IMPORTANT NNB. He dressed hurriedly, his body complaining bitterly about the prospect of another hike. But his dream seemed to have promised help, unlikely as it might be, from this canine trinity, from these returned exiles. And his visions – or dreams – of the previous day appeared to have had some truth in them too: he had found it hard to sleep mainly because of returning memories, snatches of childhood; his uncle the priest in his bedroom, kissing him, his uncle taking him away from home to live with him in the priests' house, his uncle in a big room, teaching him to walk in a funny way, men laughing as he stumbled in the dark...

He ruined me, and I am re-begot
Of absence, darkness, death; things which are not.

George hobbled to the door and opened it. The dogs charged into the living room and tore around, crashing against the cupboard, leaping on the futon, delirious with homecoming. The Alsatian jumped on George, her front paws hitting him in the chest. The bloody dogs are back all right, he thought, stumbling against an armchair, plopping into it. He rose, staggered to the door, shouting 'Walkies!' The three dogs scuttered out past him, down the steps, across the forecourt, past the goats' compound.

The foursome set off up the steep ascent beyond the animals' enclosure, a widening gap between the first three and the last. But the Alsatian frequently stopped to look back and make sure that George was still coming. If the dogs were going round a bend on the path, which was bordered on both sides by scrub oak forest, the Alsatian returned to him, and George, already breathless, felt obliged to reassure her: 'OK, OK, I'm coming.' Then she bounded off eagerly, turning to look again just before disappearing from his sight.

Tessa was looking at herself in the wide wardrobe mirror of her bedroom in her father's house. She stayed with her father once a week, because he lived alone. Sometimes she remained longer, when her husband was in one of his bad moods.

Tessa was a strange girl. Brought up motherless by a divorced father who had physically punished her sporadically but mainly indulged her whims, she was wilful by temperament and respected neither the norms of the ordinary folk nor the aristocratic propriety of her aunt and uncle, the Marchesa and her capable but silent husband. Her childhood apartness had begun at the local *scuola materna* and continued right up to university, which she had recently abandoned in mid-degree to marry a local charmer, the son of a furniture store manager, whose silver tongue seemed to offer an escape from her boring course of anthropological studies to a life of luxury and long holidays on the Riviera, and it was only now that the reality of a woman's entrapment in the rural Italian scheme of things was being borne in on her.

She always went to her father's for a day or two over Christmas, because he had no one else, but this time there was the additional reason that her husband had beaten her on Christmas Eve, having come home drunk and found neither Tessa nor his lunch. She had delayed in the city over the shopping, and he had attacked her perfunctorily, as his God-given right, when she finally returned and asked him to help with the shopping bags.

It is nothing too serious, she reflected, as she examined the bruise on her cheek from her husband's open hand and the faint stripe remaining on her thigh from his belt; but I will fix him for this. I will fix him good and proper, with some poison mushrooms. I will mix them in with his pasta sauce.

The house was old and rickety, with no central heating, and her teddybear-strewn bedroom was enormous, but Tessa did not feel the cold. Having finished the examination of her wounds, she was still looking in the mirror, and beginning to like what she saw. The faint morning sunlight, coming in through a massive window, moulded her naked body in golden allure. Although her breasts were very full, they were firm and rounded as cantaloupe melons. She saw that nothing sagged in her, no flab around her waist or on her thighs. And her bellybutton was tucked in so neatly, and her bottom so athletic and trim! But the texture of her skin above all, so velvety and sheer in this faint morning light – it was quite indescribable, really: she began to fondle herself, responding to the desirability her eyes saw in her body; then she took hold of a big teddy bear lying on the floor and pressed it to her breasts. She liked herself and wished she could find someone out there to confirm her self-liking. Not her husband, though – never again.

A thought of George entered her mind. There was some attractive power in that man. He was well-built, strong and handsome, even if a bit plump and untidy and not dressed very well. He was an intelligent man; an intellectual, like her father. He was a big teddy bear, *in fatti*. And she knew he liked her; he hadn't been able to keep his eyes off her the night of Rogero's soirée. It would be quite an adventure to have an affair with a foreigner, a *straniero*, in this close and narrow-minded community. Some night I will go to him, I will cast my sorcery on him. I will show the dull citizens the freedom of my spirit. They think I'm a *putana* and I'll prove them more than correct, just for spite. And my silly uncle and aunt, the Silent Engineer and the Mighty Marchesa, who think I'm too common and vulgar, will raise their eyebrows even higher than ever.

Aroused at the idea of sexual scandal, Tessa threw herself back on the capacious feather bed. Clasping the huge teddy bear to her breast, she closed her eyes and thought of George.

It finally dawned on George that the dogs were taking him on the same route he had walked the day before, but in the opposite direction. He recognised a house with a sign projecting from its gable, declaring *Forno Antico*. This was a rival agritourist establishment to Rogero's, one which advertised its traditional stone oven. He had heard that it was run by a family from Milan, but it now seemed deserted: maybe its proprietors, having received no bookings for Christmas, decided to return to their relatives for the holiday. They were obviously strange people, these Milanesi, because they thought they could hang up traffic signs signifying 'No Parking' and 'One Way' on the trunks of the scrub oaks, on a dirt path in the middle of a self-seeding forest.

It was a faintly sunny day and George knew that he would soon leave the scrub oak behind and the scene would open out to hillocky pastureland and vineyards, but the road would begin to disappear, revert to rock, and the ascent grow even steeper. He braced himself for the added effort, wondering in a simple, desperate faith how far the dogs were taking him. It was surprising that the Alsatian had not come back to him for some time now.

When he got to the break in the forest, he couldn't see

his charges up ahead. Not a sign of them anywhere on the rock-rough excuse for a road, right up to the visible summit. Tumbled fields to the right, a vineyard and a copse of cypresses to the left. Something white gleamed through the copse, perhaps a wall. Then he heard the barking.

As he groped his way up the path, the barking intensified, until it sounded as if there were at least a dozen dogs involved. Among clumps of withered broom, he saw a small track leading into the cypresses, and the dogs were at the end of it, standing on their hind legs at a small white gate. He broke into a gasping trot. '*Giu! Giu!*' he shouted. 'Get down!'

The dogs were putting on a great show of bravery, seeing as they were protected by the gate from whatever they were barking at. When George reached them, he saw two other dogs on the far side – *pastori abruzzesi*, half-savage white sheepdogs. They were a couple of meters from the gate, edging threateningly closer. Not one of George's trio paid the least attention to his commands and curses. He tried to pull them off the gate by the scruff of the neck, but they leaped up on it again.

The gate was a side-entrance to a large, shadowy courtyard. After an eternity of eardrum-rupturing din, a tall man in grey jacket and trousers appeared in the yard, spoke once and sharply to the white dogs, who retreated out of sight. Babs, Giorgio and Carinosa instantly fell silent, dropped from the gate and slunk away.

'*Ben trovato*,' the tall man in the grey suit said to George. 'Something told me you were coming.' He opened the wicket gate. '*Prego*, do come in.'

'Haven't I met you before?' asked George, puzzled by something tantalizingly familiar in the thin, pinched face of his host, who shook hands curtly and withdrew his own as if George's had been hot.

'Possibly. On the other hand, you may be confusing me with my twin brother, who is a little more sociable than I.'

The man assumed an air of ushering, and George understood from the vague gestures that he was to go from the courtyard and through a very large, dim living room with tatty sagging armchairs, mahogany bookcases, and a large open fireplace like Rogero's, on which burned a solitary log.

'Your twin brother?'

'Yes. The Marchesa's husband. Perhaps you have met him? The architect and engineer.'

'Ah. I met him once,' said George.

'He is Marco. I am Piero. And your name?'

'George.'

They moved on to a bright conservatory with a riot of tropical plants mixing a green shade into the soft sunlight. A couple of wicker chairs stood at a small table that was topped with colourful ceramic designs of the zodiac. The man indicated one of the chairs.

'Would you like a cup of tea – or perhaps a beer?'

'A cup of tea will be fine.'

The grey one evanesced. George sat down and looked out through the glass. He saw a driveway leading to a large wrought-iron gate, among many cypresses: he was at the front of a very sheltered house. An SUV was parked on the driveway. There were a few pots of winter lemons on a veranda just outside the conservatory. Probably brought out for an airing because of the mild weather, he thought, and wished that such ordinary observations could become the sum total of his thoughts for the rest of his life. If I ever get out of this mental mess, he promised himself, I will content myself with the simplest of things, like seeing lemons growing in a pot, in their own shining, selfless way, in the middle of winter, life continuing despite everything. He was close to tears when his host returned with a tray.

'I brought some milk,' he said, 'but I must say I have never understood the idea. Of taking milk in tea, that is.' He produced a sound that could have passed for a truncated cough or a stifled titter. 'I take it you do use milk?'

Without waiting for a reply, he slipped out the door of the conservatory, coming back with a lemon. He cut a slice and dropped it into one of the two cups in which teabags trailed their labels over the rims, on string. He poured hot water from a jug.

'The tea ceremony,' said George.

'No doubt you, likewise, find the Italian way with tea amusing?'

'Oh no, not at all. I find what you are doing so...so beautiful,' George whimpered.

The grey-suited man sniffed dismissively, sat down opposite him, sipped his tea. George played with the string of his teabag, lifting it up and down to make the brew stronger. His hand shook as he added the milk.

'You are obviously very upset,' said Piero.

'I am at the end of my tether,' George said, choking back the sobs. 'Your English is excellent. Why were you expecting to meet me?'

'Thank you. I just had a very strong feeling. I didn't know it would be you, of course, but the moment I saw you, I knew it was you. I trust I am being sufficiently obscure?'

'You had an intuition?'

'If you wish to call it that. Such a portmanteau term, covering a multitude of absurdities that have befallen me since I came to this valley.' Piero suddenly lost his composure, raised his eyes to heaven and muttered something angry. To George it sounded like an obscenity in an unknown language.

'I recognised the dogs, of course,' continued the Italian, taking hold of himself. 'Am I right in saying you are a guest of the Irish man and the German woman down the hill?'

'We've been there since September actually. We... I am spending a year there.'

'How unfortunate.'

'I beg your pardon?'

'It is I who must beg your pardon. I was thinking of something else – a professional matter.'

'What is your profession?'

'Let us say that I am most unlike my mathematical scientific brother in the respect that I have delved in very different, less precise, fields of knowledge. I was a professor of psychoanalysis and now I profess something else. I think you know what I mean.'

'You say you knew it was me that you had the feeling about, the moment you saw me. Why?'

'I could see immediately that you were haunted.'

'I am haunted,' George confirmed wholeheartedly. 'I have been haunted ever since I came here – by visions, hallucinations, voices, strange coincidences. Because of them, my partner has just left me and gone home. For all I know, this may be another hallucination, more elaborate than all the rest.'

'I hope not,' smiled the professor, taking a quick sip of tea.

Suddenly, from above them, came a shrill unearthly squawking, a warble of disappointed evil, that caused George to start upright, hitting his knee against a leg of the table, rattling the crockery. The professor managed to catch the milk jug before it toppled.

'Don't worry,' he said, rising. 'It's just my peacock has got on the roof.' He went out and made some admonitory noises, a sort of mantra. Another squawk-warble, then a flapping of wings.

'But tell me this,' he asked, sitting down again. 'For how long have you been aware that you were sexually abused as a child?'

George dropped his cup and it spilled and smashed on the terracotta floor.

'Yes, yes, I know. I know these things from years of experience,' the professor addressed the unspoken question irritably. 'Never mind the cup. You have been a *sleeper*, as it is called in the literature. There are some who never wake to their early abuse. Their lives turn out badly, but they never know why. Others, like you, don't wake to it until quite late. In your case, coming to this valley seems to have been the catalyst. You might have kept it bottled up your whole life through. You would probably have drunk yourself to death.'

George winced at a sudden significant glance from his host. 'But how do you know all this?'

'I've just told you – from years of experience,' snapped the professor. 'I look at you and see traces of sexual abuse in your features, your facial expressions, in the way you comport yourself. *How* I know this is immaterial. The question is, *What are we going to do about it?*' Piero looked at his watch. 'But I can't go into it at present. I'm giving a lecture on paranormal phenomena in Orvieto this afternoon, and my daughter is driving me there.'

Rising abruptly, he went out to the parlour and called: 'Tessa! Tessa!' He returned and said to George: 'I must go and get ready. Please excuse my irritability. I have my own tormentors. But why don't you come back around the same time tomorrow? In the meantime, write down some of the memories that are returning to you. It will help.'

'Sheorge! You are here?' Tessa appeared at the entrance to the conservatory.

'I see you two have met before,' Piero remarked dryly, and left.

Tessa looked as if she had just come from the catwalk. The first thing George noticed was the plunging neckline of her black dress. It could hardly be called a neckline at all, plunging almost to her navel, exposing demi-spheres of her breasts. Enhancing the look-at-me message, a wide-meshed web of small white pearls, like breath-freshening mints, covered the exposed skin. As if to compensate for this large expanse of pearl-dappled flesh, the black dress was long-sleeved and fell to Tessa's ankles. Her hair was dyed brunette and parted in the middle; at the front it was combed conventionally down the sides to below her ears, but the back of her head was flounced with clusters of unruly, trampish curls. Her classically beautiful features were enlivened by delight at the unexpected physical presence of the man she had fantasized about a few hours before.

George had been standing, ready to leave, but at the sight of Tessa he felt a sudden weakness, and incongruously sat down again. He had experienced an almost overwhelming impulse to lunge towards her and nibble at her web of pearls. But even seated, and ravaged by conflicting emotions, he was transfixed by her.

'You are not glad to see me, George?' Tessa said poutily, sitting down beside him. 'You look like maybe I am a ghost.' She was taking off her high heels and putting on a pair of flat shoes she had brought with her for driving.

'Oh no, Tessa, no,' George mumbled. 'Not at all, it's not that at all. Not that. It's just that...'

'You are one of my father's *clienti*?'

'It's all very strange, how I came to be here, and now you are here. You look beautiful.'

'Thenk you.' Tessa glowed with pleasure. 'You are handsome man, also.' Her face darkened. 'But I must tell you this. My father is – how you say it? – very *amaro*.'

'Bitter?'

'Beeter, yes.' She lowered her voice. 'He very beeter because he lose *posizione* in Rome university. Someone else, a woman, she take his work. In a not nice way. Now he go to other side, for vendetta. He want to know magic. Talk with spirits, I don't know. Is *multo pericoloso*.'

'Very dangerous.'

'Yes, is very dangerous. I have fear. For him. Also for you.' Tessa reached out her hand and touched George's.

He stood up, not trusting himself to observe the decencies.

'I must go.'

'Let me kees you goodbye.'

She rose and placed her arms on George's shoulders, pressed her lips on his. This time, George wasn't able to resist. His mouth responded against his will. An enormous well of hunger and delight bubbled up inside him, a geyser erupting from under the ice. There was a warm place where he had to be, to which he was invited; a centre of gravity in Tessa, towards which he was propelled. He put his arms around her, drew her body closer.

But now it was Tessa who pulled away, looking quickly towards the entrance to the living room. 'Not here, George. We go now. I see you again.'

George got up late the following morning, after an unusually deep and dreamless sleep. He sat in an armchair, having coffee. For a change, he was feeling good: the taste of Tessa's lipstick was still on his lips, and with every taste of the lipstick came a thrill of delight and a little replenishment of confidence in himself and the world. He wanted the taste of the lipstick to be there for ever. Such a beautiful young woman, he thought – and she likes me! And not only did she like him, but her lingering kiss showed a hunger for him. She is as hungry for me as I am for her, he reckoned. Where will it all end? I don't care!

It was then he noticed a folded sheet of paper lying on the tiles. It had obviously been pushed underneath the door. It took him a long period of dreamy gazing before he focused on the possibility that it was a message. Even then he ignored the paper, because it was late in the morning and he needed to jot down a few notes for Tessa's father, the irritable professor, who might put him standing in a corner if he hadn't done his homework. He found an envelope among some magazines and maps beside the television, and jotted down some points from childhood memory on the back of it:

— *Uncle comes into my bedroom when I am playing Stations of the Cross at wardrobe mirror – Jesus Stripped of his Garments.*

— *Tells me it's mortal sin to be looking at my body in mirror, but he can absolve me. Penance will hurt me a little, but Jesus suffered too for our sins.*

— *Uncle takes me from home to priests' house – claims he will look after me because my behaviour v. disturbed.*

— *Blind Man's Buff – he twirls me round, blindfolded, in middle of room where there are other men. I am supposed to try to find door. Whatever man I head towards gets me.*

— *I escape from priests' house. Uncle comes for me again but I attack him. Uncle leaves. I tell mother everything. He disappears from my life.*

George wrote down these points without any emotion: it was indeed his homework, it had to be done, but he did it thinking mostly of Tessa. The dogs really hit the jackpot when they brought me to that cypress-surrounded house, he thought: they have fetched me not only a therapist, but a beautiful mistress.

When he had finished, he turned his attention to the sheet of paper that was lying by the door. It was a message from the landlord:

Yesterday you took the dogs for a walk and then left them to find their own way home. This was highly irresponsible behaviour on your part, as the dogs could have worried sheep or got into even worse trouble. In future you are not to walk the dogs under any circumstances, and if there is any recurrence of this, or similar negligence, I will immediately terminate your stay.

Rogero McGinnes

PS Last evening, an elderly priest called looking for you. Says he's your uncle.

George was sitting in the same chair in the professor's conservatory as the day before, trying to calm himself. He selected one of the lemons on the veranda to stare at, the one that caught the sunlight shiniest, holding the promise of a perfectly ordinary future when, some day, he would look back at all this and laugh, which seemed impossible unless he could be reassured of the continued, second-by-second existence of the simple pure bright yellow shape of a lemon. He had told the professor about the postscript to Rogero's note, and it had usurped the day's agenda.

'You see, my uncle is dead. He died about a year before I came here. Please, professor, don't tell me he's able to come all this way to haunt me.'

'Rest assured, it is not the spirit of your uncle,' Piero said.

'But how can you be sure?'

'I believe what's happening to you here is the work of a child-ghost…'

'A poltergeist?'

'I prefer to call it a child-ghost, because this one is not your classic poltergeist. It does not make as much noise, and seems more intelligent than most poltergeists. But let's call it a poltergeist for the sake of accord. As you probably know, poltergeists are ghosts of babies, young children. They are mischievous – you could almost say playful, but playful in a way that would frighten most people to death. They are also typically resentful. Early death, being shut out of life's feast. They are attention-seekers; they want their tragedy to be known. They also want to make things difficult, spoil the party, for the living. They are tricksters.'

A long pause. The professor sighed a few times, cast his eyes to heaven, mouthing silently. Then he said, 'I have long been of the opinion that there is a child-ghost – poltergeist – active in this valley. But I have so far been unable to determine its source. *Non habemus corpus*. We do not have a body. However, my guess is that, in your case, we have this independent entity, typically a poltergeist, interacting with what we might call your own inner poltergeist, the Trickster in the Jungian sense, the repressed complex that has messed up your life in its efforts to break through to the surface. This ghostly trickster has been attracted to the inner trickster in you, and it has in fact acted as midwife to your repressed memories.'

'But how does this spirit know about me and my uncle?'

'This is terribly hard to explain, but the research shows that these beings seem to have some kind of privileged access to the innermost depths of people's minds. They are able to hack into and download their secrets, as it were, even secrets that people have kept from themselves, and rework them into audio-visual spectacles.'

George was looking at the lemon again. 'I'm afraid to go back in case it really is my uncle who called,' he confessed. 'He might return...'

'If you're afraid, you can stay here for the night,' the professor said gently, with a trace of condescension. 'Tessa will fix you a bed in the spare room.'

'Thank you, I'd like to.' A faint taste of lipstick, a brightening. Mettle more attractive.

'Of course. It will give us the opportunity to talk some more. It is high time you unmasked your demons.'

George didn't particularly want to unmask his demons just then; it was all too much. He wanted to go off somewhere alone and think of Tessa. He made a shift to get up, gesturing towards the sun, which was enlarged and red, hovering above the cypresses out front.

'I'd like to take a walk...before it gets dark...'

Piero put out his hand peremptorily.

'By all means, but before you go, I need to explain something about Tessa. She is my only child and I love her dearly. Her mother left us not long after her birth. I have done my best for her, with the aid of various relatives and nannies. Now she is in her middle twenties, rather spoiled and flighty. Very self-willed. I am afraid I have rather encouraged her to remain a child. But of course she isn't, is she? Getting married was a big eye-opener. Her husband is beneath her in intelligence and class. Extremely jealous, a violent type as it turned out. Every now and then, he beats her and she comes back to stay here. As a result of all this, she is hungry for notice and affection. She may prove to be – how shall I put it? – free with her favours.'

George's hackles rose, sensing the threat to the one positive in his present existence. 'Why are you telling me this?' he asked.

'Why am I telling you this?' the professor repeated with heavy irony. 'Why indeed? Ah yes! It's because Tessa and you may be a danger to one another in your present state. I observed that she was – shall we say? – glad to see you last night. Apart altogether from the problem of age difference, neither of you are psychologically stable. It would be a recipe for disaster. And I will not be able to help you in any way if you become entangled with my daughter.'

'Of course you are right,' George fibbed in an onset of diplomacy. 'I'm sorry about last night. It was a lapse.'

Piero seemed satisfied. 'It was Tessa's lapse as much as yours. I have spoken to her. Go and take your walk before the sun sets. Supper will be at eight.'

Supper was a rather tense affair, a matter of small talk, silences and surveillance. Tessa had done bruschetta for starters, followed by baked cannelloni and a tiramisu. Her presence provided the intoxication, in the absence of anything but water to drink. She was dressed casually, but that didn't stop her breasts from announcing their presence to George's starved male gaze in the constant shape-shifting of her floppy sweater as she stood up, walked, reached for things and served, leaning over George's shoulder, leaning on George's shoulder ever so slightly, defiantly flirtatious under the severe eyes of her father, who was watching every move, every exchange of glances, watching George watching his gorgeous daughter, who had looked to be coming back home to Papa from her violent husband, but now seemed in danger of being taken away from him again by another mess of a man. Ironically, this particular mess was a client; it would not do at all, and yet there was Tessa, disobeying his rules, preening herself under the infatuated gaze of the guest, fondling her kiss-curls coquettishly. She is quite a catch, her father thought bitterly; how she can manage to serve everything without a hitch and at the same time go through a programme of teasing, and keep the conversation from dying completely, is beyond me. But perhaps I am just a jealous old man, he concluded with even greater bitterness.

After supper, Piero showed George to his room. It was a small, cramped space. There were wide shelves full of books. Stacks of books and journals also covered the floor, except for a path leading to the single, neatly made bed and a chair beside it. There were fresh white linen towels at the end of the bed. A large teddy bear, wearing a smock, sat on the pillow.

'I'm afraid this is Tessa's little joke,' said the professor, picking up the teddy bear. 'You may wish to shower, or have a rest?'

'I think I'll take a shower. I didn't get a chance before supper.'

'The shower is at the end of the corridor, on the left. I'll see you in the living room when you're ready.'

George sat in the chair beside the bed, took off his shoes and socks, thought better of taking off anything else until he reached the bathroom, realised he had nothing to change into, wondered was it pointless to have a shower, decided it would at least help keep him awake during his session with Piero. He got up and took one of the towels from the bed. At that moment, there was a faint knocking on the door, a whisper. He opened the door to Tessa.

'I am wanting to tell you, Sheorge. My father say I must go stay with friend tonight. He think maybe we sleep together.' She smothered a giggle.

George stood there, delighted to see her, disappointed she was leaving, unable to think of anything to say.

'But I leave you teddy bear,' whispered Tessa. 'To remember me.'

'He took the teddy bear,' said George.

'Oh, he is so *cattivo*! Then I give you something else to remember me.' She took George's right hand and put it under her sweater, on her left breast. She held it there for a while. George felt the nipple hardening on his palm. Tessa took his hand out and kissed it.

'Another time, I come to you, Sheorge. Some night. Soon.'

Piero directed George to an armchair on one side of the log fire, and went rummaging somewhere in the dark. He came back with two large candles and a wax taper, placed the candles on either side of the mantelpiece, lit the taper from the red-hot log.

'I prefer firelight and candlelight to electricity. In any case, these candles have a special scent, very sacred and protective.'

'This is like something out of *Dracula*,' George said.

'*Dracula* is not as fanciful as some may think,' Piero replied dryly, wheeling an armchair to the opposite side of the fire. 'Did you forget to write down your memories for me?'

'I didn't. I just hope I brought the page with me.' George

searched his trousers pockets, placed his hand on the breast pocket of his shirt. 'Ah, here it is. I wrote a few points.'

The professor took the notes, put on his glasses, and read by candlelight. He handed the envelope back to George and said, 'Please tell me this. Did you love your uncle?'

'Did I love my uncle? How can you ask me that?'

'Try and stay calm. I am not asking how you eventually felt about him. Take your time.'

There was a prolonged silence, broken by a hiss or a crackle from the log. Shadows darted around the fire flames and candle flames, unquiet ghosts. The professor waited, an angler in the lake of darkness. Finally George spoke.

'I suppose a bad love was better than no love at all. In the beginning, it was being cherished, it was attention. I was starved of affection, and my uncle showed me plenty of affection and attention as long as I let him have his way. The kissing and touching were like affection, too. And he made me feel special because he kept telling me how beautiful I was, such a perfect body I had, no one was like me in the world. On the days he was going to see me, he said, he woke up feeling on top of the world. I was a little treasure, he said.

'But then I began to behave like a little treasure with other boys in school, and I quickly got the name of a sissy, a nancy boy. I got into fights. I was insatiable, I couldn't get enough attention. I even began to flirt with a male teacher. I became more and more disturbed.

'There was a huge gap between being with my uncle, where I was treated like a cherished concubine, and the rest of my life. My mother was totally unaware of what was going on. It was too unthinkable for her.

'Sometimes it happened in the church sacristy, after I had served at his evening mass. Sometimes it happened in my room, practically under her nose. But she would never for a moment suspect my father's brother, a man of the cloth, a surrogate father. She thought he was teaching me something in there. How right she was.

'Away from my uncle, I didn't know what to feel. My feelings were scrambled. I didn't know what was going to make me cry, or what would drive me into a fury. And then, he came up with his diabolical little plan. He would take care of me, he told my mother. A few weeks in his presbytery would sort me out, he assured her. She allowed my uncle to take me.

'But his attitude changed as soon as he got me away from home. One night he brought these mysterious men. I was not allowed see them – my uncle pretended it was a game of blind man's buff. It was the game of blind man's buff that the Roman soldiers played with Jesus, when they were mocking him after the crowning with thorns. I was suffering like Jesus for the sins of the world. But I was sick and bleeding that night from so much violation. I told my uncle I didn't like the game of blind man's buff, that I didn't want the sufferings of Jesus except with him, and he got very angry and hit me. After a few more nights of these mysterious men, I ran away. My uncle came to our house looking for me. I hit him smack on the face with a stick of firewood. I wanted to kill him. I actually broke his nose.'

'You felt betrayed by your uncle?'

'Yes, I was deeply hurt and raging inside. It was his betrayal of our little love-nest together that upset me. I suppose I knew in some way that he no longer cherished me; it was no longer him and me special, I wasn't his little treasure any more. He was grooming me to be anyone's little treasure. He had become my pimp.'

'And how do you feel about this at present?'

'I don't feel anything. Relief, maybe – that I can talk to someone about it. It's not really me to be talking like this.'

'That's because you've spent your life in denial.'

'It doesn't fit with my macho image – to have been abused to such an extent,' George said wryly. 'To have been such a fairy.'

'You are simply disparaging yourself to give it such a name. These things happened to you, and now they are part of you.'

'Are you saying I'm really deep-down gay?'

'What is wrong with being gay? But no, I'm not saying that. As a child, you were sexualised by your uncle as a passive male recipient of active male sexual attentions, and this orientation has stuck in your psyche.'

'Not any more,' said George decisively.

'Ah, so!' Piero hissed. 'You think that my excitable daughter will rescue you from the psychic wounds inflicted by your uncle?'

'Something like that,' George said with dull hostility, guiltily glancing at his right hand, the one that Tessa had placed on her breast.

'Your relationships with females have not worked out, and will not work out until you confront your childhood abuse. Has it ever occurred to you that your current status of deserted bachelor strongly suggests that?'

'I prefer to think it's more a matter of meeting the right person. That it's a case of having a passion strong enough to bury the past.'

'No, my friend, no. The energy you have invested in your uncle will continue to assert itself. Typically, you will continue to wax hot and cold. You will go off the female scent and pick up the narcissistic one which provided your uncle with a feeding frenzy of abuse. And you will continue to re-enact – I am guessing here, maybe in front of a mirror, since that is where the whole affair began – your role as your uncle's little plaything.'

George turned his face away. He had an uncomfortable flash of memory – Barbara coming into the apartment bedroom to see him nakedly cutting shapes at the wardrobe mirror. When he looked again, Piero was in his by-now characteristic pose of eyeing the ceiling, muttering incomprehensibly.

'What you need, my friend, is to take your situation seriously,' he said at last. 'I can see you are not a fit subject for psychotherapy – not at the moment. My daughter is obviously a complicating factor.'

There was another prolonged silence and this time George was sulkily determined not to break it. The fire no longer glowed and the chill of the night had advanced right up to the hearth.

The professor laughed humourlessly, rose from the chair. 'I wanted to get away from complications. I find it most ironic. Most ironic indeed. I wanted to retire gracefully, and raise horses. What you need before anything else, my friend, is insight, an epiphany. But I cannot arrange that for you. What I can arrange, however, are a set of circumstances which, if you come to them in the proper frame of mind, will lead you to see your situation in that very beneficial light which is known as epiphanic. But alas, having the proper frame of mind has presented itself as your current big problem. Therefore I very strongly advise you to abstain for the foreseeable future from drink and from sexual entanglements of any kind but particularly with my daughter. Let us try and get some sleep.'

Barbara had to wait so long in the waiting room of her consultant's private clinic that she became uncomfortably conscious of her heartbeat, a strenuous pumping under her breast, and she thought to herself, Yes, I'm definitely over-active again; and no wonder, with all I've been through. But when she timed the pulse by her watch, there were only eighty or so beats to the minute.

She had tried reading a magazine and given up: news of the Queen, of the Princess Diana cult, of royalty throughout the world, the romances of celebrities, of opera singers and rock stars who had finally managed to pull their lives together, who knew that their latest companion was for ever... These magazines were considered appropriate in doctors' waiting rooms across the globe, as if medical opinion had divined an occluded connection between being sick and living vicariously; but now that she thought about it, Barbara was convinced that living vicariously was the worst illness of all, and accounted for a large number of physical ailments. Take, for example, the television-watching couch potato who dies of a heart attack...

The waiting room was old decency – antique-looking shabby furniture and old-fashioned wallpaper with classical motifs. Barbara had sat on an armchair whose springs were broken so that it almost swallowed her. She had to clamber out of it and sit on its hard front edge, and with that immobility of people in doctors' waiting rooms, she didn't go to find a firmer seat as people thinned out around her, but remained bumsore on the hard edge, passive now because everything depended on the results on the doctor's desk, on thyroxin levels, TS3s and TS4s, and that other figure, for TSH, which she couldn't quite understand but was a kind of harbinger looking into the future.

People talked very little in doctors' waiting rooms. They were in no-man's-land; they had turned off the switch for living, much as you turn off the gas when you go on holidays. They were waiting for permission to continue living, and you knew by their abstracted looks that they weren't behind their faces at present; they were out. Barbara realised that she probably had the same kind of blank expression as the others. An ancient clock, its face peering from a wave congealed in wood, ticked solemnly on the marble mantelpiece, giving her the impression that her limbo was of a definite, measured, but unknown duration; a limbo whose span was measured by forces beyond her control.

But time doesn't move in a linear, progressive way; various present tenses, like picture slides on a carousel, flick into place, sometimes unexpectedly sudden in their arrival. When it seemed to Barbara that the picture of the waiting room was stuck, immoveable, the carousel flicked to the consultant's office, and there was the consultant, standing behind his desk – tall, gaunt, bespectacled, myopic, conveying his usual impression of suppressed energy; breezy, falsely jaunty, dismissive of irrelevant details such as how his patients actually felt; now sitting behind his desk again after a lightning handshake.

'Not my problem,' he said with a quick smile when Barbara had answered his mantric How are you? with a complaint about constant tiredness, listlessness. 'Your levels are perfect.'

She had rehearsed a mental list of symptoms accruing over the past few weeks – since the fracas with George – but now they evaporated, like water off the shell of a boiled egg, or a tornado off a weather-monitoring screen. She felt proud, as if she had won a prize, been awarded a silver or bronze medal in the Olympics of Health. She began to feel better, and by the time the consultant had finished explaining the figures, translating the values of nuclear medicine on the report that had been sent him by the Italian hospital into the more familiar, conventional ones Barbara was used to, she felt decidedly better, energetic even. The doctor waved her a breezy goodbye, and she was ready and eager for what lay ahead that afternoon: a visit to the National Gallery, an hour or so looking at pictures, followed by meeting her mother and Alan in a café near Piccadilly, and taking Alan to the cinema.

She came out of the clinic into a bright, cold January day, and headed for the train. On the journey to central London she thought of many things. She was pleased that Alan had asked to go to the cinema; it was a sign, perhaps, that he was recovering his zest. And she herself was regaining her interest in life with every passing minute. Her next appointment with the consultant was in six months' time; she was certain a lot would happen in six months. For a start, she would organize an exhibition of the work she had done in Italy: a modest, local show, perhaps, somewhere in her mother's locality; an affirmation of what she had done in the few months before the break-up, a record of the change that had come over her painting through confronting her phobia. Purely for her own satisfaction, of course; though it would be nice if a few of her school colleagues attended, even bought something. And if she succeeded in persuading some institution to put on the exhibition, that might even be a spur to doing more pictures, a deadline to work towards.

Suburban stations came and went, people got on and off the train. Taller buildings began to appear, standing out here and there among the others in her vista from the carriage window, giving a deceptive impression of less density. Now she was thinking of a painting she wanted above all to see: 'Weeping Woman' by Picasso. She wondered was there at least one of its many versions in the National Gallery. She hoped there was. But if necessary, she was prepared to go to Barcelona or Madrid. She had changed quite a bit, to be so eager to see a Cubist painting. The idea that had just come into her head seemed perfectly crazy. Perfect but crazy, crazy but perfect. She wanted to do a pastiche of Giorgio as Picasso's Weeping Woman.

There was, of course, the small matter of George and Rogero. She would let it resolve itself. She had been given a clean bill of health, and was certain that the New Year would be very special.

It is now the beginning of February. George and Rogero are both in the right mood for their first remarkable encounter. Rogero is digging furiously in his garden, as much from frustration as from purpose, digging a drill for potatoes, but the drill is already far too deep, more of a trench, a grave for his hopes. After much guilt-motivated procrastination, he has just contacted Barbara on the phone to give her the names of the spurious documents which she would be kind to look up and photocopy for him in the British Museum, and she has been brisk and businesslike with him, not a hint of a trace of a longing to dally in conversation. She will be glad to do the photocopies, and post them on and goodbye. Thank you for calling.

He is digging the grave of his hopes, a drill for the new potatoes. All he can hope for now is Mathilde and spuds, and to cap it all, though he doesn't know it yet, who should be coming along the road with his own dark thoughts, who but the Man on the Hill, his leman's rejected lover who still hovers, is still in with a chance, obviously, given the curt treatment Rogero has just received from the Madonna of his Sunset. Either that, or neither of them has a cat's chance in a tsunami, a snowball's in hell, neither George nor Roger, who are, on the contrary, condemned to be alone together, each a reminder to the other of their respective failures to follow the scent of happiness to its source.

George's dark mood, as he makes his way along the Round-in-Reverse, now passing Wuthering Heights and heading for the flat final stretch towards the field and the house and the garden-uprooting Rogero, is compounded by several professorial injunctions. Apparently in preparation for some arcane moment of manifestation, considered by Piero to be indicated in the circumstances of his case as the groundwork for a remaining lifetime of psychoanalysis, George is to abstain from intoxicating liquor for an indefinite period; for exercise, he is to walk ten kilometers every day; and he has been given a mantra to mutter in the event of a visit from his uncle or the putative poltergeist or indeed from both simultaneously. He is also to report to Piero once a week, and stay away from Tessa.

Apart from all that to darken a man's already-dark mood, Tessa has been proven a flirt. She has gone back to her husband, for the sole reason that he had the neck to call on her at Piero's with a bunch of flowers and a bunch of high-flown, meaningless Italian male apologies. And George has also become more aware, with every treacherous step on this rocky descent, of the great hole in his heart that is the absence of Barbara; the absence that Barbara already was before she left couldn't compare with this, her physical absence: one of the twin columns that held up the remains of his life has collapsed, and brought everything else down with it, except for the other column still standing in a desolate and lonely place, a monument to Barbara-less, Tessa-less nothingness.

By the time he comes round the final bend on the flat stretch, and sees Rogero mullucking in the garden earth, George has lined up the dominoes of every dead thing in his existence on this earth: his father's absence from his childhood, his avoiding, ineffectual mother, his abusing uncle, his non-existent literary career, the absence of the woman who was his surrogate mother, the absence of the woman who was to be his sexual redemption, and finally the presence of this gravedigger furiously wielding his spade, rival for his surrogate mother's affections, Oedipus's deadly landlord-daddy.

'God bless the work,' George shouts with pugilistic stage-Irish sarcasm. Rogero freezes in his shabby work attire at the sound of the unloved voice, his hands tightening on the spade. George walks on. He has stepped a good twenty paces before Rogero unfreezes and runs after him.

'Just a moment, you!'

George doesn't like to be just-a-moment-youd. It is a cornerstone of his residual dignity not to allow himself to be just-a-moment-youd. The phrase, together with the clipped landlordish tone in which it is uttered, conjures up the whole history of colonialism back in the Old Sod. He swings round and squares up to his just-a-moment-youer, who is still holding his spade in both hands. The two of them, there in the sunset, against a background of winter garden, where withered tomato plants still droop on their bamboo supports, and a grave has been dug, present a tableau of imminent murder.

'I do have a name, you know,' George says with quiet menace, keeping a cautious eye on Rogero's tightly gripped shovel.

'Well, you can take your name with you elsewhere in six weeks' time,' Rogero says. 'Unfortunately, I am obliged by your tenancy agreement to give you six weeks' notice. But I will be informing the police of your mental instability, and they may well decide to pre-empt things and send you packing much sooner.'

'You asshole!' roars George. He makes a sudden forward movement, then thinks better of physical assault. Rogero steps back, holding the spade higher, in defensive readiness.

'How convenient,' George resumes quietly. 'Get me out of here, and then you can invite Barbara back and have her all to yourself. Isn't that it? But first you'll have to get rid of your wife, won't you?'

Rogero blanches. 'How dare you make such allegations. You need psychiatric help.'

'And so do you. You've been seeing my uncle, and he's dead.'

'What on earth are you talking about?'

'Your little landlordly note of a few weeks ago. The PS you added to your warning about my canine neglect.'

'What do you mean, a PS?'

'Surely you know what a PS is. Your postscript saying that my priest uncle had come looking for me. And he's dead. He's been dead for almost a year.'

'I most certainly did not put any postscript on my note to you.'

'You most certainly did.'

'I most certainly did not. This is your diseased imagination.'

'Do you want to see it? I've kept it. Maybe I can use

it to prove that you're the one who's seeing things. It's up in the apartment.'

'I don't need to see it. I know what I wrote. And there was no postscript about your uncle, simply because there was no uncle. You need to be committed.'

'You miserable little shit. Let me show it to you.'

George bounds up the steps and into his apartment. The landlordly note is in a drawer of the cabinet under the television. He unfolds the note and looks.

Not a PS in sight.

'Sherlock Holmes and the Case of the Vanishing Postscript,' Piero said. For the first time in George's hearing, he laughed heartily. 'Oh dear me, dear me.'

'I'm glad you find it funny,' George sulked.

'My dear man, if you had been the victim of as many pranks as I have been since I came here, you would probably have developed a taste for the more original ones, among which this is definitely not to be counted.'

They were walking up and down the veranda outside the conservatory of the professor's cypress-secluded house in the late afternoon sun.

'How long does it take to become a connoisseur?'

'Sarcasm, George, sarcasm.' The professor wagged his finger in mock reproof, and chuckled.

'I hope you don't mind me saying so, but you seem in unusually good form.'

'I note the word *unusually* and no, I don't mind you using it. It is true that I am in unusually good form. I myself have also managed to arrange a nice little prank. On an enemy of mine. It is a form of justice, of course. Where there was no justice.'

'You mean revenge.'

'Precisely.'

The professor paused to pluck a sprig from a bowl of oregano set on a pedestal, sniffed it appraisingly.

'Revenge, I find, is a very satisfying feeling. Don't you think? Nothing fatal, of course. Just enough to even things out.'

'When I broke that bastard's nose,' George reminisced, 'I didn't feel any satisfaction. That was because my mother made such a to-do of it. *Oh the holy priest, shame on you, George,* and so on. I didn't hear the end of it, even when she finally accepted that my uncle had abused me and was quite the opposite of holy. It was as if what I had done to him was worse than what he had done to me.'

'The problem with child abuse is that it's taboo. Society multiplies the victim's sufferings. As if the abuse wasn't horrific enough, it is usually surrounded by denial, silence and stigma. But you're darkening my mood.'

'So I have a counsellor who doesn't want his mood darkened.'

'I'm sorry, George. It was a joke. But your remarks were leading me into therapy, which I have ruled out for the present.'

'What is this intervention you spoke about? You haven't told me anything except that it's on its way. It's all very vague and woolly. I don't know what to expect.'

'Neither do I,' admitted the professor. 'But my success in this little matter of retribution gives me great confidence. Obviously, retribution will not meet your case, as your uncle is dead. It will be something of immense value to you, however; depending, of course, on your adherence to the regimen of preparation. It should sort you out, maybe not once and for all, but at least enough to benefit speedily from therapy.'

'It's taking ages. You know I have to move out of my apartment in a month.'

'Don't worry. I am very confident now. I know that my standing with my supplier is good.'

'Is that all you can tell me?'

'I can add a few more points. Firstly, you needn't be expecting another of the crude, melodramatic types of visions you talked about. Retro-gothic stuff, the staple of our little poltergeist. What I can offer you will be something far more subtle. I spoke to you before of an epiphany. It's not that I can bring you an epiphany, of course – as if I was an epiphany man in the same way as the man who brings ice cream around in his jingly musical van is an ice cream man. You must be your own epiphany man.'

'And where do you fit in?'

'Let me continue this analogy. There is some truth in saying that I will bring you the ice cream, but if you are not an ice cream man yourself, in a different sense of the phrase – that is, if you don't like ice cream – then I, as the driver of the jingly musical van, will stop in vain outside your front door. However I think you are an epiphany man in this sense of being capable of realizing an epiphany, because you are a searcher for meaning in your own life, all the more so since you came here; you became intensely concerned to rescue yourself from the fate your childhood seems to have foisted on you. But there are habits and attitudes you have built up over the years that militate against your liberation. And of course there is the added complicating factor of your attraction to my daughter. Because of these it is always possible that the epiphany, when it comes, will not be to your liking – to continue our ice cream analogy, it could be the wrong flavour for you. Hence the absolute need for the regime of abstinence, chastity and physical well-being that I have prescribed for you. The regime will make you more open to what the epiphany reveals, more ready to accept it, in whatever flavour it comes.'

'That gives me some idea of what you're getting at,' said George. 'The analogy is helpful.'

'Thank you. But I feel the comparison has weakened in being spun out. *Flavour* is too feeble a word for what I am expecting to come to you. It will be more of a jolt, it may jolt you out of your senses, but it won't be one of the melodramatic kinds of communication our child-ghost specializes in. It will be capable of reaching and healing you inwardly, not simply put you in such a state of dread and despair that you need help.'

'Can I ask a question?'

'By all means.'

'I remember what you said when you first met me: *Something told me you were coming.* Are you sure that the something wasn't the poltergeist? Maybe it planted the premonition in your mind. You know, to make you more ready to accept me.'

'Where did you get such a ridiculous idea? You're not suggesting that it was trying to help you? This trickster may be intelligent, but from my extensive knowledge of its behaviour, it plays pranks and nothing but pranks, and it plays them either to gain attention, to spite the living or to make death more interesting for itself.'

'Please bear with me for a minute. I had a dream on Christmas night in which the dogs sent me a postcard to say they were going to help me. And sure enough, they led me to you. The thought has occurred to me that the poltergeist might have sent me the dream, and could have been controlling the dogs.'

'Now you are *really* darkening my mood, George. This is nonsense. It's just wishful thinking brought about by a sentimental notion that there's a poltergeist out there that likes you and wants to help you.'

Well, it certainly doesn't like you! That was on the tip of George's tongue, but he managed to keep it in.

'I'm sorry, George. You must excuse me for snapping at you, but your naivety concerning the paranormal was beginning to rankle. And now I have to say Ciao. We meet again in a week's time. Remember your regimen.'

As they embraced curtly in parting, the notion entered

George's head that one night of love-making with Piero's daughter might be far better for him than any of her father's remedies. 'How is Tessa?' he asked as casually as he could.

'As well as can be expected. You know, of course, that she's gone back to her husband. Everything will be fine for a while and then she'll come back to me.'

'Give her my regards.'

'I certainly will. But no more, George. No more than your regards.'

Piero chuckled. He had regained his unusually good form. After all, his replacement in Rome had been replaced.

George had got into the habit of leaving the door of his apartment slightly ajar, in the faint lingering hope that Tessa would keep her promise of a nocturnal visit. One night, when he was asleep, the three dogs held a meeting in his living room. Babs, the Chairperson, had summoned Giorgio and Carinosa, the other members of the Committee for Canine Well-Being, to an EGM.

The Alsatian reclined on the fouton, Giorgio the mongrel snuggled up on the armchair, and the terrier Carinosa, the smallest, had to be content with sitting upright on an armless wooden chair with a circular seat.

'This is a sorry pass,' growled Babs.

'A sorry pass indeed,' yelped Carinosa.

'I call this meeting to order. Items on the agenda: first, the minutes of the previous meeting...'

'May be taken as heard,' barked Giorgio.

'Second, What to do about the Sorry Pass. Third, AOB. All agreed?'

'Arf.'

'Arf.'

'Okey-dokey. Let's tackle the main item, the Sorry Pass. To put it in a nutshell, there are no walkies for us doggies because all the humans are too busy plotting and ameliorating and fretting the life out of themselves to even think of us.'

'Well said indeed.'

'I put it to the meeting that we must address, first and foremost, our own canine interests. We thought that introducing yer man to the hermit good who lives in the wood might have sorted him out for dog-accompanied hikes. But it has only complicated things. Unless we are content to see a spring pass without walkies, we must do something drastic.'

'No walkies in the spring?' whined Giorgio. 'I can't bear the thought of that.'

'Take but walkies away, untune that string, and hark what discord follows,' yelped Carinosa.

'Precisely,' said the Chair. 'When dogs are not walked, extensively and regularly, all kinds of evils come upon the world. Unfortunately, however, it is always the case that when things are bad, as they are right now, they have to get worse before they can get better. So at this point in time, the question we have to ask ourselves is, *How can we make things worse?*'

'And what is worse than dogs not being walked?' Carinosa asked, in a didactic manner that strongly suggested she already knew the answer.

'I can't imagine anything worse than that,' moaned Giorgio. 'I'm getting on. I mightn't even see another spring.'

'But it's obvious! *Dogs not walking* is even worse than *dogs not being walked*. Therefore, if dogs do not walk at all, even worse evil will come on the world than if they were simply not *being* walked.'

'I don't get it.' Giorgio frowned.

'*I* get it,' barked Babs, 'and your foxy terrier logic, Comrade Carinosa, is very much in line with the course of action I wish to propose. Namely, that we have a lie-in protest against our neglect, and make such a nuisance of ourselves that yer man will be goaded into taking us for walkies. In other words, we will up the ante and respond to no walkies *for* doggies with no walking *by* doggies.'

'That will be too hard,' objected Giorgio. 'Did you ever see a dog staying completely still for five minutes, unless he was asleep or suffering from depression? We are by nature restless creatures.'

'You weren't very restless the night the burglars came here,' yelped Carinosa.

'Don't let's get personal now,' Babs cautioned. 'None of us was very restless that night. They must have drugged us.'

'But I need exercise more than either of you. I might get a stroke.'

'You can exercise without walking, Comrade Giorgio. This is no time for prevarication. I put it to the committee that in our own best interests we commence without further notice a lie-in on the balcony outside, of indeterminate duration or until such time as walkies are restored to us. All in favour bark once.'

'Arf.'

'Arf.'

'Arf. Motion carried. Any other business?'

'Is it all right to take a blanket or something out of the apartment to lie on?' asked Giorgio. 'My old bones, you know...'

'In the circumstances, I think it is justified to take a few items to lie on, and to cover us. After all, there were supposed to be three humans here, and now there's only one.'

'There's a small matter you have both forgotten about, smart and all as you are,' persisted Giorgio. 'How are we going to *eat* if we stay on the balcony all the time? Is this a hunger strike as well as a lie-in?'

'If yer man doesn't throw his leftovers out on the balcony,' Babs said, 'we may slip down for a few minutes after dark to our master's lousy bowls of pellets.'

The dogs languished. They slept on George's balcony by night, settling themselves on wicker armchairs or bedding down on the stone floor. (George's overcoat had become Giorgio's undersheet and was growing a crop of mongrel hairs.)

By day the dogs lay round the balcony, pathetic, hovering between hope and despair. They stretched in stupors against the parapet as rain invaded the floor and formed a widening pool in the middle. As George came and went, they opened depressed eyes and closed them again. Occasionally, he tripped over one that was lying in innocent ambush on the threshold; he would turn back, cursing, and dislodge the abject canine flesh with a push of his foot. But the dog would lie down again, a little farther from the door.

The dogs got on George's alcohol-thirsty nerves. He kept tripping over them, the pleading of their eyes tugged at some painful nerve of guilt and unreality. He felt guilty about hating the dogs, hated them because of his guilt. He was continually on edge because of abstinence and waiting. Despite the professor's optimism, and his own vigilance, there hadn't been anything that remotely resembled an epiphany, no set of circumstances a shade out of the ordinary that quickened in his mind towards significance.

George had nothing better in proximate bodily form to feel guilty about than three dogs; no woman any more to feel guilty about, no child. That kind of guilt would have been real, would have helped to define reality; but this kind undermined definition and reality. The dogs did not complain, did not react. There was no agreement breached, no social contract dishonoured by ignoring them. They weren't his dogs. Those other two lunatics downstairs should be looking after them; his canine responsibilities had been revoked. And yet they looked at him with those depressed or pleading eyes, Giorgio innocent and depressed, Babs pleading and eager, the small Fox Terrier catatonic. The constant presence of the dogs was for George like the unhappiness of hell, as defined in the terms of scholastic theology, because it amounted to the possession of that which he most hated and feared. His hatred of the dogs intensified his hatred for the landlord; if this monster in human shape had felt any appropriate concern for his pets, George would never have been attacked in the core of his being by canine *angst*. The immobility of the dogs was yet another twist to his continuing ordeal; but Piero had dismissed his discomfort as a symptom of alcohol withdrawal.

One day, out of all patience, George lifted the inert canine lumps and carried them one by one down to the bottom of the balcony steps, with scatological warnings about their daring ever to return. But when he woke from his afternoon doze and looked out through the glass of the door, they were, as he feared, back again, a triptych of sprawling misery, three mafiosi guarding the gates of sanity against him.

Rogero couldn't believe his ears: the female voice at the other end of the line was warm and welcoming.

'Oh hello, Rogero,' it said. 'Did you get that stuff I sent you?'

Poor old Rogero had had a terrible day. It was one of those awful days when he had to stay at home with Mathilde. There was no way out of it. His wife had insisted that she was in no fit condition to meet the people from the tourist authority who were coming on one of their regular inspections; she would be staying in bed, in fact, because she didn't feel at all well. How convenient, Rogero thought to himself that morning, but what he said was 'Very well, dear. Shall I bring you some coffee?'

He had settled down in the living room to mark a pile of overdue essays. He worked agonizingly slowly, with little concentration, and waited for the tourist people to come. Normally he would have done these assessments in the college library where the ambience was more pleasant, the distractions more eye-catching; normally he would have had a morning lecture. But life with Mathilde was not normal. And he, though he was the villain of the piece, responsible for what had happened to her over the years, was not a normal villain. A normal villain would not, for example, divide his life between his crimes and their voluntary expiation; he would leave the expiation to others, or to the dubious hereafter, and take his chances. But poor old Rogero's perverse sense of justice demanded not only that he make satisfaction for the past, but also for the future. He accepted these frightful hours of wading through reams of spidery handwriting and waiting for unreliable unpunctual visitors who would undoubtedly prove difficult, in a dark house permeated with the presence of an implacable sufferer, on a cold day of incessant rain, as punishment in advance for what he was going to dare that night.

And so he waded all day through the spidery handwriting of the predictable essays, taking a break to prepare lunch for himself and his patient; waded on into late afternoon, until the veils of rain drifting past the window merged with the handwriting of his students, until reading the essays was like trying to read the rain, the soul-destroying script of the rain. Initially, the hills outside the window maintained their contours, a grey slightly darker than the grey of the sky, but as the afternoon wore on, the separation became less and less tenable, a purely notional one, like the separation in merit between one humdrum dissertation and another.

The expected visitors never arrived. But otherwise things progressed despite appearances; the evening and the essays passed into darkness, and soon it was time to burn a log in the huge open grate, time to prepare supper.

The slow flame in the grate grew like the meaning of Rogero's self-punishment. The whole point of the exercise was to push back the boundaries of Mathilde's suffering by spreading the empire of his own. Now, unlike in the morning, it was Rogero's suffering that filled the living room; Mathilde's had retreated down the corridor and was presently confined to her bedroom. The day of expiation had created a space in which Rogero could act. He brought Mathilde her separate supper. Too nervous with do-or-die intent, he ate nothing himself. He waited a judicious amount of time, drinking a judicious amount of whiskey, watching the flames climb in the grate, listening to the patter of rain on the window panes. Then he pounced on the phone before the retreating aura of his day's misery shrank to dimensions in which action was impossible…

'Yes, thank you very much,' Rogero replied to the voice on the other end of the line. 'I got the offprints a couple of days ago. They were extraordinarily useful. It was so kind of you to take the trouble.'

'Not at all. It wasn't any trouble. I'll be glad to get some more if you need them.'

Rogero was gobsmacked by hope. This was going to be difficult, not like the countless smooth-talking phone conversations of his past, with students and young assistant lecturers, in which he arranged ambivalent assignations. This was make or break, but he needed to keep his head a little longer, not sound over-eager. Well, he was allowed to sound eager, but not eager for Barbara.

'That's what I wanted to talk to you about,' he said. 'In fact, the material you sent me was so interesting that it's whetted my appetite, as it were. I want to read up thoroughly on the subject. So I've decided to come to London myself, and spend a few days in the British Museum.'

'Oh, that's nice,' was the reply, in a neutral tone, but not entirely discouraging.

'I thought perhaps… well, I thought we could meet up sometime for coffee or lunch. That is, if you're not totally put off by the idea after what you've been through over here.'

'Oh Rogero, not at all.' To his immense relief, the voice at the other end was still friendly, its warmth now mixed with a trace of amusement. 'All that wasn't your fault. It was very good of you to let us stay. But when are you coming to London?'

'Well, actually I was hoping to go over in a few weeks' time,' Rogero ventured blindly, not knowing how on earth he could manage to get away.

'That's fine. I'll be here at my mother's. Why don't you phone me when you get here?'

'I certainly will,' he blurted. Then, to cover the traces of emotional slippage: 'Say hello to Alan for me.'

'Do you know, you seem to have been a big hit there. He often asks about you.'

'What can I bring him? What kind of present do you think he'd like?'

'Oh, anything at all, coming from you.'

'Well, goodbye till then, Barbara.'

'Bye, Rogero.'

Rogero simply had to finish the call at that point. He couldn't trust himself any further not to come out with something incongruous or revealing, although he wanted to prolong the erotic excitement he felt at the sound of Barbara's voice. He felt unsatisfied when the phone went dead, experienced a kind of *coitus interruptus*. Yet as he remained sitting by the phone, drinking whiskey, a sense of triumph suffused him. He had dared to act, and he who dares wins. Persistence pays off. If at first you don't succeed...

Obviously there were many more hurdles to jump, but the race had begun. He had been wise not to mention George's misdemeanours and his imminent eviction. That would all come out in due course, in a moment of greater intimacy, when he would explain that Barbara and Alan were more than welcome to return to the apartment. He began to fantasize moments of greater intimacy, and fell asleep in his armchair, exhausted by a phone call.

Remo the melancholy innkeeper was glad to see George again, and George was glad to see Vecchia Romagna again. Remo had poured two generous measures, and explained that the drink was on the top of the house, because he was so happy to 're-see' his friend.

Enmeshed in a mental debate about the rights and wrongs of breaking the abstinence imposed by the professor, George swallowed the brandy and his glass was refilled. The debate with conscience continued, however; the issue of drinking or not was still alive, because lo and behold there was the full glass in front of him. There may have been a bump in time, but the fact was that a full glass of brandy stood on the counter in front of George, untouched. He began to relax, and this was necessary, if he was to broach a rather sensitive matter.

There was an air of dereliction about the Etruscan's bar, the pallor of a dull day in early spring on the glass surfaces, on the tinsel of Christmas that hadn't been taken down, on the unsold boxes of *panettone*. For a while, George listened dutifully to Remo talking about his son and daughter-in-law and grandchildren who had come on a visit from Bologna during the long-gone festivities. Eventually, he felt relaxed enough to interrupt the innkeeper's ramblings.

'Excuse me, Remo, but I need to discuss something with you.'

'*Prego*, my friend. What is it?'

'You are obviously a good family man, and of course there are many good family men who keep their true sexual orientation secret... Let me put it another way. I don't really have any problem with this, but I just want to ask you a very personal question, if you don't mind.'

'Please. You are my friend. We do not keep secrets.'

'Did you by any chance, and forgive me if I'm wrong, but did you by any chance proposition me the last time I was here? You know, before Christmas?'

'What is this word *proposition*? I do not understand.'

'Did you want to have sex with me before Christmas? Are you gay?'

'What you saying to me? I want *sesso*? With you? Before Christmas?'

'Please don't be upset. But I seem to remember that you exposed yourself to me. You showed me your thing… You showed me your *cazzo*.'

'I show you my *cazzo*? Before Christmas?'

'Yes. Do you remember you sent the people away, you told everyone to go home and you shut the bar? Then you showed me your *cazzo*.'

'I never showing you my *cazzo*. *Macché*, why I show you my *cazzo*? You friend. I not *finocchio*, you not *finocchio*. We friends.'

'I am so sorry…'

'In Italy, men give more expression to lave,' Remo continued. 'Maybe I kees you, maybe I touch you, but I do not show you my *cazzo*. We friends, OK? If you want, I am showing you my *cazzo*, but not in *omosessuale* way. Maybe you not sure if I am *eunuco*, have no balls? Like Hitler?'

'Were I a man, that I were one, I needs must know,' quoted George.

'*Non ho capito*. What is this you are saying?'

'Oh nothing. It's from the poem I'm trying to remember. That line has just come to me. But no, I certainly do not want to see your *cazzo*.'

'I forgive you, my friend, because you have too much imaginations. Maybe because you is poet. Maybe because you is drinking too much.'

The melancholy innkeeper laughed a little and then emitted a deep sigh, a sigh that swooped on the already dim bar like a thick layer of twilight. 'But for me there is no imaginations. All is too true. I am *kaput*. People not come to my bar any more because I kick them out, to be with you, my friend, before Christmas. They say I lave a *straniero* more than *Italiani*.'

'That's awful. I'm really sorry.'

'*Non importa*. I go *in pensione*. I put *Vendesi* on bar.'

'You're putting the bar up for sale?'

'For sale. You teach me better English. Maybe no one is buying, but I have many, much many. But what is many?' Remo gestured a broad hopelessness. 'What is to do with too much many? Let me show you something.'

Remo opened a large red binder which lay on the counter, a stamp collection he had been glancing through before George arrived, and began to turn the stiff pages.

'You see this,' he said, pointing to a large commemorative stamp, Hitler on one side, Mussolini on the other, the globe between them. 'Because of these two, I keesed my youth goodbye. And then my wife, she dies –'

'My woman has left me, too. She left me all alone here, before Christmas. She wasn't carried out, in a coffin, like your wife. She left of her own motion and volition. She left me because of the shadow in my mind. She left me because she thought the shadow had no substance. But, as the poet put it, if there is shadow, a light and body must be there.'

'Now you go away in your imaginations again, and I cannot follow you.'

'It's quite simple. I was abused as a child. Sexually. By a priest who was my uncle.'

'Yes, it is so sad,' reflected Remo in a matter-of-fact accepting way that surprised George. 'It is so sad, this *sesso* with the childs. This was also to me when I was little. My *infanzia* was taken, then came Hitler and Mussolini, then my wife died, then my children they go away, and now...'

'Who abused you, Remo?'

'My cousin. But later I have my vendetta.' Remo's face glowed with the rare memory of a satisfactory outcome. 'We have a fight. I break his nose. He break my nose. Then he try to shake my hand, and I break his arm. Nobody say nothing. *Finito.*'

'Good for you, Remo! I also broke my uncle's nose.'

'Then we really are friends, because many things happen the same. *Salute.*'

Another bump in time, and the full glass remained full.

'Roger, I want to speak with you. Immediately.'

It was Mathilde – who else could it be? – a chiaroscuro figure in the opening to the corridor at the other end of the living room, as Rogero entered the apartment, home late after a long day at the university.

'Surely it can wait, whatever it is,' he replied wearily, leaving down his briefcase. His anger rose as the monotonous unhappiness of his situation defined itself: to work like a dog all day, and then come home to this. 'Can't you see I've just got in? Some of us have to work, you know.' He went to the kitchen alcove to brew himself some coffee.

Mathilde now did something that was quite unlike her; instead of waiting, imperiously, insufferably, for Rogero to come to her, she crossed the living room to where he was crouched in the alcove, searching for the coffee pot.

'What is the meaning of this?' she shouted.

Rogero turned his head, his nose meeting the plane ticket in Mathilde's outstretched hand.

'You have deceived me, Roger. You are going to London,

to see that woman.'

Rogero got to his feet, brushed past Mathilde and went to the dresser with the glass door, for his Courvoisier. His mind raced as he hastily splashed out a drink. He remembered that he had written a B, and Barbara's telephone number, on the outside of the paper wallet which held his plane ticket. *Why did I do that? Why did I not hide the tickets? How can I have been so insanely stupid?*

Mathilde was standing beside him again. He sensed the shaking of her body.

'To think that I married a beast. To think that I am living with a monster,' Mathilde screamed, her words half-strangulated by huge convulsive sobs.

This is it, Rogero thought with the sudden clarity of decision; this has to be the end of it. No more false pretexts, no more false explanations. He left the filled glass on the edge of the ponderous ancient dresser, and turned. For the first time, he faced Mathilde's implacable misery, the living projection of his own unnameable guilt, with a fortitude not supplied by alcohol.

'I'm not a monster,' he said, clearly, calmly. 'It's just that I'm not a saint.'

The words struck. They were death, because after them Mathilde went strangely quiet, her trembling stopped. For a long time she looked quietly at the unflinching stranger in front of her, the bearer of her death warrant. When she spoke again, her voice was calm and businesslike, in the manner of dictating a last will and testament.

'Very well then, Rogero.' She hadn't called him Rogero since the beginning, the good years. He felt the twinge of regret, and felt it pass. 'Very well then,' she repeated. 'You know what must be done.'

'But Mathilde...' Rogero remonstrated feebly; he no longer had the energy for it.

'You know what must be done, Rogero. You must take me to the Home. The time has come. You must arrange it before you go. Please make the arrangements tomorrow. And you know what I must bring with me.'

Mathilde left him, crossing the living room with dignity, dying with dignity, born to endless night. She was briefly framed in the opening to the corridor, disappeared into the dark.

Rogero reached for his glass of Courvoisier and drank it in one gulp. It was done; one desperate lunge at happiness had at least brought him clear of misery. He lit a late fire, sat for a long time by the glowing log, reflecting on Freud and the purposes of forgetting.

Barbara, at her mother's home in a London suburb, is working on her cubist pastiche of Giorgio. She kneels on the floor of her bedroom, a coffee-table art book to one side of her, open at a reproduction of a Weeping Woman, her Italian doggie notebook on the other side of her, open at a sketch of Giorgio's head; a large drawing pad in front of her, open at a blank page. She covers sheet after sheet of thick art paper with acrylic markings and tosses them impatiently aside. It is not coming, she thinks in despair, it is too difficult; what a crazy idea it was – crazy and stupid, stupid and crazy. She bursts into tears, thumps the floor with her fist. She gets up and sits on the bed, muttering 'It's hopeless – hopeless! Who the fuck do I think I am?'

But there's something in her that won't let go. Day after day, the same morning routine: a tense breakfast when she snaps at Alan for some small heedless act such as dropping a spoon or pouring the milk carelessly over his cornflakes, so that it ricochets out over the bowl and on to the tablecloth. And when Hilda intervenes in defence of the child, she growls at her mother. She actually growls. Then she goes up to her room and begins again: sheet after sheet of thick art paper covered with demented markings and thrown aside.

Hilda hasn't experienced so many conflicting emotions for a long time: she is simultaneously a widow still in mourning, a fretting mother, who is beginning to be afraid of and for her daughter, and a doting grandmother, joyful and energetic at the very sight of Alan. Every morning she takes her grandson by the hand and walks him to the school bus. Every evening she collects him at the stop, takes him to the shops, and indulges him with chocolate, ice cream and toy cars. Occasionally, she brings him with her to the local library. She sits him down with a story book or comic, goes to the desk and asks to speak to the head librarian, who has an important role in her plan to rescue her daughter from snarling insanity.

'Why is Mum always so cross?' Alan asks her.

'It's just that – well, she's an artist, you know. Don't worry, dear. She'll be fine again in a little while.'

Barbara will not let go, and something eventually begins to emerge on the white paper: a darkness that is in one version Giorgio the dog and in another the obsessed person she has become in developing her art. She is aware of a growing talent in her hand, in the turn of her wrist, which is a frightening gift from the recesses of her grief.

Will you ever be the same again? her timid ego asks, as the dog and the woman come closer, become one.

The headlights of Tessa's SUV, which George did not see, cleaved the dark. The roar of the engine, which he did not hear, ploughed through the silence. George neither heard nor saw Tessa; he felt her. As he woke, she was already astride him, her lips reaching out towards his in the pitch black bedroom.

'Sheorge, wek up,' she whispered. '*Sono Tessa. Tutto bene.* I am fucking you, Sheorge.'

She was flute-music shaken out endlessly, the seduction of wind-notes in hollowed wood, an infinite blowing of multi-coloured bubbles, the cream rising to the top of the milk. She was the Rapture repeated over and over. She was its brief footnotes, the whispered pillow talk. She was the rise and fall of life's breathing. She was Jove's lightning bolt from the blue, the glint of which never quite leaves the eye.

She was the key that opens the door of the pleasure dome decreed in Xanadu. And dawn was the Person from Porlock, the thought-police knocking on the door.

She kissed him once more when it was over. *Goodnight Sheorge. Sweet dreams.* But he had passed out.

George woke on a cushiony plateau of clouds. He was borne aloft on them. His body was singing the gentle song it used to sing after tumultuous, abandoned sex with Barbara, the song it hadn't sung for years. He wondered if it had all been a dream, but the plateau of cloud-cushions he was resting on, the song his body was singing, rebutted his quibbling intellect with undeniable finality. Tessa, an absolute smasher, a *bomba*, had come to him in the middle of the night and fucked the bollocks off him.

He lay in fulfilment's reverie for a long time, gazing on prospects of unbounded promise: of happy explosive sex, of a home in Italy with olives, vineyards and noisy happy children, of a muse to provoke the masterpiece of his later years, which would puzzle the critics by its youthful exuberance because they had never known sex with the likes of Tessa.

When he finally rose, he found that the living room table had been cleared except for one clean cup in the middle, in which rested a teabag. Leaning against the cup was a folded piece of paper on which was written *Niente Latte. Tessa xxxxxx* The kettle on the gas stove had also been filled, and George lit the gas ring under it. The afterglow of pleasure suffused his body, and he walked through the rooms, humming to himself, as he waited for the kettle to boil. In Alan's former room, he discovered that the desk had also been cleared and prepared as if for the act of writing: his reading glasses to one side, a pencil and notepad on the other, the computer at centre back; nothing remained to clutter movement or hamper thought. Tessa didn't know that he wasn't writing, of course. But she would become his new inspiration.

The absence of milk was irritating, but Tessa, although Italian, obviously knew it was important to him – hence the note, almost by way of apology: as if to say, I'd have gone and got you milk but I must scoot back before my husband knows I'm gone. And the six kisses! He counted them again and his heart soared.

The kettle began its whistling crescendo. George picked up his cup and brought it over to the stove, in readiness. He reflected that he had never caught a glimpse of Tessa last night. But he had felt her, oh by God he had, every inch of her, and she felt the way she looked, the way a woman like her would feel to the touch of a man. Pure silk.

But what if it wasn't Tessa?

George poured his tea, picked the teabag gingerly out of the cup with his fingers, and went back to the table to re-examine the note. *Niente latte. Tessa xxxxxx.* Mercifully, it hadn't disappeared, like the horrible PS.

A loud male voice began shouting somewhere outside. He couldn't hear clearly what was being said, but one of the words sounded like his name.

He rushed out to the balcony and looked all around, but there was no one to be seen. There was nothing to be heard, not even a sleep sound or groan from the dogs sprawled beside him. It's the woodcutters over in the forest, one calling to another, he thought, pleading with himself against the rising terror, against the countryside's blank desertion.

He hadn't noticed it at first, but there was a taxi right underneath the balcony, beside his Toyota. It was only then his ears picked up the purr of the idling engine. Probably waiting for one of the two monsters, he thought. A swarthy head poked out of the taxi's window and stared up at him from under tufty black eyebrows.

'Signor George?' asked a dry cracked voice.

'Yes?'

'I am told to take you where you need to go.'

'To Piero's?' George asked.

'No, not to Piero's'.

'But I have an appointment with Piero,' George protested, finding it hard to pull his eyes away from those of the taximan.

'I am taking you to another place. You will know when you see it. Get in, please.'

The command seemed to supply the required act of obedience, because George had descended the steps and was sitting in the front passenger seat beside the driver before he had exercised any act of decision. The taximan drove away furiously, made a screeching handbrake turn on the gravel, as if to emphasise the urgency of his mission.

Rogero waited below the balcony until the din subsided. There was somebody knocking, repeatedly, frantically, on the glass panel of the door to George's apartment.

'Hello up there! Hello?'

Piero had walked down the hill to Rogero's place in the hope of finding George there. He went to the edge of the balcony, stepping over the supine dogs.

'Ah, it's you, Professor Marco,' said Rogero. 'What can I do for you?'

'I am Marco's brother, actually. I am looking for George – I don't know his surname – George, your tenant.'

'He is no longer my tenant. Or at least he ought not to be.'

'I am worried that he may have gone missing.'

'Why don't you come down?' Rogero was uncomfortable with this above-below exchange, seeing that he was in the inferior position. When Piero came down, however, he did not ask him indoors. A hostility towards anyone who could be concerned with George's well-being simmered beneath his briskly polite manner.

'George often goes missing, both mentally and physically. I'm afraid I must tell you that I've had rather enough of his antics. I've given him his notice. But he's obviously still around.' Rogero motioned his head towards the red Toyota. 'He would hardly leave without his car, would he?'

'I believe he is in grave danger. He hasn't kept an important appointment and it may mean that he...'

'It has nothing to do with me,' Rogero interrupted, forgetting his civility.

'I believe it may have a great deal to do with you,' Piero retorted, and was immediately startled to have said it.

'What on earth do you mean? I have a very troublesome tenant, whom I am forced to evict, and you're saying that I'm in some way to blame? My dear sir, I'm not very interested in this conversation. Good day.' Rogero went back indoors.

Piero stood there, puzzled with himself, wondering where the accusatory comment had come from that had riled George's landlord. He was about to leave when he heard a voice above him.

'The hermit good who lives in the wood is here, searching for yer man.'

171

He looked up and saw Babs and Giorgio, leaning their forelegs on the parapet, not looking at him but out over his head, like two humans taking in the expanse of countryside at their leisure. Animals that talked were not entirely new to Piero; nonetheless, a tremor of dread passed through him.

Carinosa, too small to imitate the stance of the other dogs, now jumped on to the wall and sat beside them. She, too, directed her gaze at the scenery.

'But yer man has gone on his perilous journey,' continued Babs, as if she was speaking to the woodland and the olive groves.

'And yer other man – our master – has been found out by our mistress,' said Carinosa. 'Aren't we kilt entirely from listening to the desperation in her voice?'

'Things have got worse, so,' said Giorgio. 'That means they're soon going to get better, and walkies will be restored to us. I presume that's why we have abandoned the lie-in protest against our neglect.'

'It's also because we have to be with yer man in his hour of need.'

Out of the air, Babs produced a tobacco pouch and Rizzla papers. She began to roll a cigarette.

'You see, yer man has been taken on a circul*arf* journey,' she began explaining to Giorgio, as she pulled a wad of tobacco out of the pouch.

'Surely you mean a circular journey?'

'No, no. I mean what I said. A circul*arf* journey is a typo journey that is almost circular, falling just short of returning to its point of departure. It is a tad short of being a full circle, and as a result allows us doggies to have walkies in order to reach the destination.'

'Walkies for doggies at last!' Giorgio barked ecstatically. 'I can sniff new scents in the air. Spring has arrived, the best time for walkies.'

'Tonight's hike won't really be walkies in the strict sense

because we'll have to go unaccompanied,' Carinosa cautioned. 'We must disobey our master for the sake of a greater good.'

'But why is yer man being taken on a circularf journey?' Giorgio asked.

'He needs to be foxed to be more terrierfied.'

'He has to plumb the depths of desAlsatian.'

'Will he have to cross the border of the collie-active unconscious?'

'He will.'

'And how far from circular is this circularf journey?'

'About five kilometers. He's been taken by what is very much the scenic route to the ruined church on the mountain. He won't get there till after dark.'

'Ah, God, this is the life, surely!' Babs lit her roll-up and took a long drag. 'We'll be setting out pretty soon, on the arf of the circle. It is incumbent upon us as friends of man. We must do what we can, come up with a plan.'

Piero hurried away, shaken, muttering to himself. Rizzla papers, roll-ups, the arf of the circle. For pity's sake, what next? He tried to dismiss the talking dogs as a bad joke, but a heavy sense of foreboding thwarted the attempt.

The taximan drove in silence, and George certainly didn't feel like small talk. They kept to minor roads, and were very shortly out of George's familiar surroundings and driving through villages and small settlements, up and down mountains, hugging forested precipices and sudden clear drops where a river flashed in the depths. If he had been in a receptive mood, the passenger would have enjoyed the scenery: the blue-grey Appenines, furred by forestry, the folds like flesh-folds of huge animals, the fur still flecked with snow. But on this particular trip, the animal appearance of the mountains only fuelled his baleful fantasies.

Time passed, and they were down on the level again, on a windswept plain. On one side of the road deserted villages clung to slopes of rocks, ghostly white walls with eyeless dark of windows, decayed buildings, abandoned homes, villages of the dead, of vampires, of werewolves. The mountains now lay like huge animals in folds of flesh on the other side of the plain. The car was shaken and buffeted by the wind, the roaring wind that blew in this huge, desolate space.

'Where you from?' the driver barked suddenly, shaking George out of his melancholy. When he looked for some sign of engagement, however, the taximan was eyeing the road intently as if he was driving through fog, as if he had never spoken.

'I said where you from? Why you not answer?'

'I'm from Ireland,' George volunteered meekly. 'But I have been living in…'

'Why you come here?'

'I needed a break.'

'You need a brek? Why you come here if you need a brek? Why you need this brek?'

'From writing.'

The driver took his eyes off the road, looked at his passenger for the first time since the journey began. 'You is writer. You need a brek. And you come here.' He emitted a dry, cracked laugh.

'I'm sorry now that I ever came.'

'Is too late.'

There was a long silence. They were beginning to ascend again, and now the driver had good reason to squint intently at the road, because the sun, about to go under, was glaring blindingly down from the rim of a mountain. It was dark by the time he spoke again.

'There was a writer, *inglese*, I knowed him. He come here. He go fucking crazy.' The driver touched his temple with

a middle finger. 'He go fucking crazy, like you.'
'I'm not crazy.'
'Yes you is. You is fucking crazy. Why you come here if you not crazy? Why you want a brek? What is problem? Problem is you is crazy, then you come here, you is more crazy.'
'That's about the size of it,' murmured George. 'Professor Piero could not have put it better,' he added, to himself rather than to the driver.
'Professor Piero,' the taximan said with a tone of resigned contempt.
'You know him?'
'Yes, I know him. He also crazy.' Finger to the forehead again. 'He serious crazy. He dangerous. Now I see why you is crazy. You go to Professor Piero. Why you go to Professor Piero?'
They were speeding downwards. The tyres ratcheted sickeningly against the rim of the road. George caught a glimpse in the headlights of a yawning drop.
'Will you slow down?' he shouted, his anger spurting through at last. 'Who the hell are you, anyway? Why are you asking me all these questions? It's really none of your fucking business.'
'You want me slow down? I slow down. Is all right. We nearly there. *Calmo, calmo.* But why you go to Professor Piero?'
'The dogs brought me to him. Maybe you know the dogs, too, since you seem to know everything. And maybe you know Tessa. And Rogero and Mathilde. And maybe you know that I was sexually abused as a child, by my uncle.'
'Yes, I know everything. They all crazy. Rogero, Tessa, Mathilde, Professor Piero. They all serious *pazzi*. You bet they is crazy. Like you. Maybe the dogs not crazy – it not matter. You uncle, maybe he crazy, but he not fucking you. No *sesso*. Is all in you head, because you crazy. Is so simple. Why you

175

blame you uncle because you is fucking crazy? But we here.'

The car screeched to a halt. George could see nothing in the headlights but a grass margin and trees.

'I leave you here,' said the taxi driver. 'Is maybe two, three kilometers on *sentiero*, liddle road. It go up, up, up. Soon you see fire. Follow fire.'

'I can't see anything.'

The driver slapped his forehead in frustration, started the engine, reversed furiously, lurched forward and stopped again. A narrow path between the trees appeared in the headlights.

'Get out, please.'

George got out, suddenly changed his mind, lunged at the taxi driver, grabbing him by the lapels of his jacket and bringing his face up close to his own.

'Who are you?' he demanded. 'You better tell me, because I've had enough shit from you in a few hours to last a lifetime. Who are you?'

The taximan placed a hand on one of George's tightly gripping knuckles. He recoiled at the touch, as if electrified.

'It not matter,' the taximan said, adjusting his jacket. 'I bring you where you need to be, is all. Now I go. Now you go on liddle road. Up, up, up. Soon you see fire. Follow fire. You crazy. Soon maybe you is more crazy, or maybe you not crazy any more. *In bocca al lupo*, best of lucks.'

George watched the headlights of the car until they disappeared. As if on cue, a crescent moon came out from behind the clouds and gave him enough light to begin his ascent.

George is in the ascendancy again, in the sense that once more he is going up a hill, only this time, for the first time, he is climbing in the dark. It is night, with a mingy sliver of crescent moon just beginning to grow, but hardly beginning to glow, given that for most of his journey it is behind fast-moving clouds. This is quite an uphill battle, there is much stumbling and several falls. There are tears of rage and tears of terror, sobs of sorrow and sobs of misery. George presses on because there is nowhere to return to. There are wounds of a superficial nature, scratches from briars, nettle stings. There are curses whose volume is kept to a whisper, because George, in a mode of wishing to efface his own existence, feels that he must be quiet, he must negate himself and not disturb the night creatures in the woods on either side. There may be wild boars, possessed by demons, watching him. Gadarene swine. They would be enormously inconvenienced by a din.

He has forgotten a protective mantra given to him by the professor, some Latin formula not easily recalled if it hasn't been learned by rote, and he is whispering something of no particular efficacy, or even meaning, in the present context, over and over as he struggles upwards: *I must be more proactive in my approach. I must be more proactive, for all your sakes.*

There is an island in his head, the island of sanity, but it is fast disappearing under the waves. On this island a figure is backing towards the high ground in the centre, talking to the waves as he goes: *This cannot be happening, you should not be doing this, there is no reason for this to happen.*

An owl screeches at regular intervals, an unearthly screech, a *memento mori*. There is another sound, constant and very faint, which George now begins to distinguish: a kind of humming that becomes clearer as he climbs. He stops to listen more intently. The sound comes and goes on the wind. Is it some kind of chant? Now he sees a yellow flickering that disappears and after a while reappears. The sound comes and goes, the flickering appears and disappears. George trudges on: *I must be more proactive in my approach, for all your sakes. This cannot be happening.*

A third George emerges from between the terrified self

and beleaguered sanity: one that quickens its pace and begins to growl. The three of them trundle along in one body, in mortal combat.

'Tessa, stop the car, please.'

Piero was straining his eyes, looking out the side window into the darkness as they drove through the countryside.

'What is it?'

'I think I see a light. I can't see properly through the glass.'

Tessa stopped her SUV on the narrow road. A car honked irritably as it swerved to pass. She switched on the hazard lights.

'Do you see it?' asked Piero as they stood on the margin, staring at a tiny patch of yellow-gold flickering on the dark-on-dark hump of the mountain.

'You're right!' exclaimed Tessa. 'But there's nobody living up there. What do you think it is?'

'I'm afraid it is nothing good,' murmured Piero. 'I think I may have been tricked.'

'Do you mean about George?'

'Yes, I have been tricked. I did not arrange this. Get back in, drive along slowly. There must be a path leading off the road.'

Through the night walked a lonely hungry wolf, surrounded by a spherically shaped snowstorm. Along a mountain path in the night moved a giant glassless crystal ball in which could be seen a lonely hungry wolf surrounded by snow. The flakes of snow were fragments of a disintegrating self, the wolf was the bulk that remained of the self, from which flakes of snow continued to detach with every growl and howl the poor beast emitted. The diminishing beast, the increasing snow approached a ruined chapel lit by fire, the fire of a thousand black candles. The lonely hungry wolf emitted his howls and growls against the chanting that came from the ruined chapel. The chanting was pulling the self of the wolf asunder by causing him to howl and growl against it, to try and drown the sound. The howls and growls against the chant were flaking snowflakes of self from the wolf. The chant increased its intensity as the wolf approached, the howls and growls multiplied. By the time the snow-surrounded wolf had got to the door of the chapel from which the chant was coming, there was no wolf left in him. The wolf had become every inch a snowstorm.

The chant was tearing his soul out of his body, but he entered the chapel. In the light of hundreds of candles, placed on ledges and in crannies all around, he saw the flickering white of the faces of the satanic choristers. Disposed on either side of the altar, they were robed in black from head to foot. A figure was standing at the high altar dressed in a priest's white alb and cincture. The figure raised a hand and the chanting stopped.

As he moved up the aisle, he recognised the broken-nosed features of his uncle. 'Welcome, George,' his uncle said, stretching out his hands, his voice like a distant rumble of thunder. 'Welcome to our little diversion.'

Candelabra glowed on the high altar, and behind them were lit the high candles of Benediction. The choristers had stepped back and their white faces disappeared in the shadows. His uncle was still standing with his hands stretched out. 'Sit in the front pew, George, on the right-hand side.' Now his voice was the purr of a big cat. 'Cover your head, George.'

He sat at the very edge of the pew, on something soft. 'You're sitting on your hat, George,' a child's voice giggled high up in the rafters. From under him, he pulled out a woman's broad-brimmed hat, complete with face-covering net. Involuntarily he put on the hat. Then he remembered that when he was a child, the right side of a church was the woman's side.

'So lovely to see my little treasure again after all these years,' his uncle mocked in his cat-purr voice. 'Let us begin the frivolities.' He vanished behind the high altar.

All the time, it was as if he was heavily drugged, but nevertheless he had a very distinct feeling of an unseen presence of unfathomable evil. From his worst nightmares, he recognised the space he found himself in: a desolation of cosmic width and emptiness that now engulfed an old chapel, so that it was no longer a chapel on earth, but was inside this different cosmos. And this universe was also, somehow, a person, self-satisfied in its capacity to tear asunder, to destroy anything of human good, an enemy of kindness and love. It was a universe of hatred, envy and greed, a bad infinity self-satisfied at what a great being it was, that could exert all this power; an appalling otherness there was no way of representing materially except by the sound of those lost voices which had chanted the letting go of all comforting restraints, invited a dreadful void to come and claim the world. But Satan, having more pressing business, was only present as cosmos, not in person. He was represented by the person of this low-grade priest.

A luminous line appeared on the floor, curving around the space in front of, and disappearing behind, the altar; marking out, it seemed, a theatre of action. 'He wants you to cross the line,' squeaked the child's voice in the rafters and giddy child-laughter reverberated around the church.

His eyes were now fixed on a boy turned away from him, naked except for a cloth around his loins. The boy was making unusual gestures with his hands, but he instantly recognised them as miming the stripping off of clothes – Jesus being stripped of his garments. Then his uncle entered again, in black cassock and beret, acting out his discovery of the boy *in flagrante*, taken aback, pretending shock, finger raised to chide. But soon the priest was embracing the boy from head to toe.

His uncle looks up from his act of child rape on the steps of the high altar, laughs and says, 'Look what I'm doing to my little treasure, George. Are you angry with me? Why don't you cross the line and break my nose again? Cross the line, George.'

He felt sick and wanted to get up and leave, but he couldn't move.

'Cross the line,' the child's voice echoes in the rafters.

Now there is a circle of men in front of the altar, and in the middle of them his uncle is blindfolding the boy, twirling him round and stepping aside, as the boy puts his hands in front of him and begins to move towards one of the men. Another act of child rape follows.

'Cross the line, George,' purrs his uncle.

He is suffocating. Fear has been choking his rage, but now rage gets its fingers on the windpipe of fear. He makes an enormous effort to rise, gripping the wooden rail of the pew. It is like trying to get out from under a boulder. He stumbles against the kneeler of the pew and the netted hat falls off. Child-laughter echoes all over the church. The wolf is reborn from nowhere, crawls out of the pew, growling. *In bocca al lupo*. Best of lucks. Convulsing with every effort, he moves towards the luminous line.

His uncle twirls the boy again. He can hear the child's sobbing and pleading – Please, uncle, please. His uncle berates the boy, slaps him across the face, twirls him round once more. The boy hesitates, going one way, changing his mind, going another way. Hands stretched out, the boy begins to walk towards *him*.

'Just another few steps, George, to your moment of supreme happiness,' his uncle mocks, laughing a terrible, doom-laden laugh.

He is on his hands and knees, moving towards the

luminous line. The naked boy is standing on the other side of it. The boy takes off his blindfold.

'Kiss yourself,' says his uncle. 'Come along now, George, kiss the little treasure of yourself. Isn't that what you've always wanted – to love yourself? I was only helping you, George. I was helping you to love yourself, and they have called me a pervert, a paedophile. How misguided of them. But now is the moment, George. Now is the moment of the consummation of your self-love. Make love to yourself, George.'

'Kiss me, George, love me,' says the boy.

'*Kissmeloveme,*' echoes the child's voice in the rafters. *Kissmeloveme, lovemekissme.*

On all fours, an animal looking up at a young master, he is mesmerised by the boy's beauty. The closer he gets, the more he is drawn, body and soul, into the spirit of the infernal ritual. Instead of wanting to attack his uncle, he wants to embrace his boyhood self. And now it seems easy to move. He is crossing the line.

Suddenly, three dogs erupt on to the scene. They rush up to him, barking furiously. He has put a hand over the line, but before he can ground it, one of the dogs has sunk her teeth in his wrist, and he screams in ordinary, innocent, hallowed human pain. The dogs bark at him, grip his clothes in their teeth, pull him away from the enchanted circle. Meanwhile, his uncle's voice is thunder directly overhead: *Cross the line, George! Love yourself!*

The shadow of his beautiful young self begins to fade. The shadow of his uncle begins to fade. The choristers have come into the light again, resuming their terrible chant. The dogs are tugging him down the aisle. Everything fades.

Light, like the first light on the deep, broke on George's eyes.

He was lying on the grass. Grass like the first grass. The first dog, Carinosa the Carer, was licking his wrist. A cure in a dog's bite, and a cure in a dog's lick.

He patted the first dog and slowly picked himself up, the first man. He was numb with cold and damp, his bones were aching, but his mind was clear. Like the first light. There was nothing in his head but morning: grass and trees in first spring bloom, light on a ruined chapel. No one there, they had all been shadows. Except for the three dogs, friends of man. They were with him. In the real world, the only world.

In his clarity he understood that what happened had not happened, not really, not in the real world, only in the shadows of the mind, in the shadows of the not-being, in the mirror of Narcissus, in the death which was the great refusal.

He said three *good dogs* – good dog, good dog, good dog – and patted the three doggy heads. It is all over, he said aloud. I was blind and now I can see. Morning light on grass and tree, on chapel empty of shadow-creatures. No more the figments of the demonic dark, of the evil otherness. No more the chanting of the voices of the lost. No more the things which are not, from now the things that are. Every day from here on is a gift, he said.

Oh the gentle grass. And the gentle trees standing in a quiet labour of leafing. Life's labour has not been lost on me, and now is the moment of my mind's and heart's rebirth. I have been warned but not found wanting. What darkened me in all my faults is revealed as the fault of another. Oh the shriving coldness of this morning, my baptism in its dew. The gentle dawn of this brave new world, and the sturdy scrubs in the thin-pillared loggias of their silence. And the silence broken only by rustlings of fellow creatures. Ecstasy to have lived to see this day. Ecstasy to have continuance from this, to have been granted reprieve, and not only reprieve but more, a bounty of future, to have been given this day, this dawn, my daily bread of fortitude and fitness to face the world.

What light shines up there ahoy, methinks I see my star approaching, the star of my being dimmed for so long has emerged of from its night of shame.
Were you there when I untied the brown paper parcel of the earth?
Were you there when I opened the brown paper parcel of the sea?
Were you there when I unwrapped the brown paper parcel of the sky?
The three dogs barked. Arffirmatively.

Piero and Tessa woke with the first light. They were huddled against one another for warmth, in a ditch, their faces wet with the dew. Slowly, achingly, they separated and stood up. Piero, wearing a great frown of puzzlement, looked down at his crumpled suit, felt the dampness of it, automatically brushed his hand over the creases.

Tessa sneezed repeatedly. Piero clambered out of the ditch, gave her his hand and pulled her up. Immediately, he bent over in a spasm of coughing. Tessa rearranged her skirt and jacket as best she could, continuing to sneeze. Lizards darted in the undergrowth, crows took flight with raucous caws.

Finally, father and daughter straightened up, gazed at one another. Finding no solution on one another's faces, where fear struggled with bewildered embarrassment, they looked at their surroundings.

Below them, the path they were standing on disappeared into scrub oak forest. Above them likewise. On either side, scrub oak forest.

'We have been fooled,' said Piero, coming to.

'Poor George,' sighed Tessa, remembering. 'If something has happened to him in that church…'

'But why have we been tricked?' demanded Piero, looking up angrily at the brightening sky. 'Why has this been allowed to happen?'

Into the small hours, they had followed the flickering light. But it had turned out to be a will o' the wisp that kept changing position, appearing in front of them, disappearing and reappearing behind them; first it was on one side of them, then on the other side. They had walked up and back down, taken narrow trails off the path and retraced them, and found themselves again and again at the same point where Tessa's torch had revealed a collection of household items, including a couple of rotting mattresses, that someone had wantonly dumped in the ditch. Every so often they could hear a confusion of sounds – shrieks, laughter, shouts, chanting… barking? – but when they stopped to listen, all was quiet except for a few creaks and rustles among the trees. Then the light had disappeared altogether and, overcome by an urgency of sleep, they had slumped in the ditch.

'What is that?' Tessa reached out suddenly, catching her father's arm. She was looking up the slope of the mountain.

Something, not very far ahead, not far from where the path wound around and disappeared, was not forest. An outcrop of rock maybe? Or a wall of some kind?

'It is some kind of wall,' said the professor. 'It may be the chapel. Let's go and look.'

'But maybe it is just another deception, another trick.'

'It is not too far. And we have no choice. We must see if George…'

They heard barking, and a few seconds later the three dogs came bounding towards them down the path.

And not long after them came George, walking with a very definite spring in his step.

'I have never felt better in my whole life,' George declared when he met his seekers, robustly hugging each of them. The professor stiffened politely in his embrace, but Tessa threw her arms around him and firmly planted a kiss on his lips.

George could not stop talking. As they ambled homewards – it must have been about seven o'clock on a cold bright morning – he blabbed to Piero about his night's ordeal, explaining its benefits in hyperbolic terms: how the terror he was subjected to had cauterised his inner wound, cleansed his mind through and through, and how the sheer relief of his miraculous escape from the evil ritual had given him a wholly new perspective on life, a determination to make good the remainder of his days. The past was behind him, and the rest of his life in front; there remained some business to be settled, but with the light that shone in him now, no task or challenge was impossible. It was not an exaggeration to say that he had been saved in a deep theological sense, and he would be forever grateful to the powers above and their instruments on earth, his five companions on this sacred morning, three dogs, a wise professor and his compassionate daughter. And of course, grateful also to whatever spirit-being had acted as midwife to his childhood memory, who had forced what was hidden to be revealed; and whatever reason that spirit-being might have had for doing so, the result was a coming to terms with the past, an acknowledgement of a lasting wound, but a moving on in the newfound light. And so George blabbered, like Scrooge on Christmas Day after the visit of the Ghost of the Christmas Future, as they made their way across the mountain and along the paths that would bring them back to the professor's and Rogero's homesteads.

Piero, of course, was glad to see George alive and well, but behind his joy and relief there remained puzzlement and resentment. Responsibility had been taken out of his hands. There could be no doubt about that. What wrong could he have committed to merit being bypassed in the care of a client? Had he grown complacent in his relationship with his unseen supplier? Or was this a very unusual epiphany, an unusual 'cure' indeed – using the powers of darkness to bring about some good? And what did the dogs have to do with it all? Where did they fit in? There were too many unanswered questions for Piero to be able to share unreservedly in the joy of the occasion.

Tessa, however, had no problem with George's high spirits – quite the contrary. She walked linking arms with him, and when he ran out of things to tell the taciturn professor, she talked and joked with him in broken English, and George responded in broken Italian. The dogs were delirious, running all over the place, tearing through clumps of broom and hedges of blackberry thickets and wild vines, departing and returning for pats on the head, for *good dogs*, then darting off elsewhere, disappearing, becoming a frenzied rustling in the hedges, shooting out into the open when least expected, startling the trio of humans, to Piero's annoyance and to the huge amusement of George and Tessa, who were by now walking with arms around one another's hips, and stopping occasionally to kiss behind the unsettled professor's back.

When they got to Piero's place, Tessa insisted on putting a bandage on George's wrist before he went on to collect his car and belongings. They were having coffee in the conservatory. The professor had excused himself and gone to consult some book or other in the library. The dogs had gone AWOL as soon as the humans had turned off the main path and towards the house. George didn't worry about them because he considered them under some kind of occult protection.

'No need for a bandage,' demurred George. 'Carinosa has already licked the wound clean.'

'Where you go now, Sheorge?' asked Tessa as she applied ointment to a piece of lint.

'I will go to London – to see the Queen,' said George, and

laughed giddily.

'You mean you will go to London to see your wife.' Tessa made a show of pouting.

'She is not my wife. She is – was – my partner. Not married, you know?'

'*Si, si.* You go to see if she still want you. How you say? Forgive?'

'No, not that. I want to apologise to her for my bad behaviour. And maybe explain about my childhood.'

'She not listen to that, Sheorge. You go to lave her, or not go *nemmeno*.' Tessa tightened the bandage around George's wrist.

'Ouch! Too tight.'

She smiled wickedly. 'You silly man, Sheorge.' She undid the bandage and began again, rolling with more care, concentrating. 'I have husband. He leave me when he like, come back when he like. He hit me when he like. Everything when he like. Now I leave him.'

'Good for you, Tessa.'

'It not good for me. What is this stupid lave?' She seemed about to cry, but laughed instead. 'Maybe I keel him.' She looked up from the bandage, looked him in the eyes. 'You good man, Sheorge. I like you.'

George reached out and clasped her wrist gratefully. 'Thank you, Tessa.'

'Why you have to go to your silly Queen?' Her eyes twinkled.

'I will come back. I have to put things right. But I'll come back.'

Tessa put sticking plaster round the bandage and slapped his wrist. Done.

'All right. You go to your silly Queen, come back, I have keeled my husband with mushrooms. No one know.' She laughed again, her breasts compromising the buttons of her jacket. George wanted to take her there and then, among the pots of lemons, to subdue her, to make her his own. His libido in full erectile flight again, he watched her laughing, head tossed back, auburn hair streaming down. Maybe his aura of having survived a hellish ritual made her want him all the more – and he wanted her more than ever because she seemed to offer pure uncomplicated happiness, because nobody who is *laved* by such a stunning woman can ever be nothing, ever feel again that he is nothing – as long as she wakes with him and lives with him and loves him each day of his life. He was about to pull her, laughing, out of her chair and into his arms when Piero, outfoxed and morose, entered the conservatory.

'I am glad you have found something to laugh at,' he remarked, pouring himself a cup of coffee.

Japanese cherry blossomed in Mathilde's garden, whitethorn blossomed in the wild. Hawkbit in the fields, the puffed breasts of small birds, blue tit and goldfinch, in the privet trees behind Rogero's house. Trees and bushes along the edge of the wood were coming into bloom, but the slim gangly oaks held out, hanging on to clumps of their old leaves. A willow trailed its pendulous first foliage down into the landlord's vegetable plot. The rosemary hedges bordering the short drive that led from the white road to the house were in blue flower. A shrillness of birdsong made infinite small punctures in the air. Flocks of pigeons alighted on George's field, the forgotten field of his visions, which had just been harrowed. The pigeons alighted and ascended again, and alighted somewhere else.

George had set off in high spirits from Piero's house to collect his Toyota. When he got to the bottom of the hill, with the young olive trees, the house and his red car in view, he paused, inhaled deeply, and stood observing the sky. High clouds, he thought, high pressure clouds, how beautiful they are. Puffballs, cotton swabs, rows of fleshy ribs. Then he noticed a transparent layer, thinly ribbed like sand on a beach, the Lost Beach of Childhood appearing up there in the sky. And when he noticed the pale crescent of the morning moon through the thin layer of cloud, he could see that the ribs were moving, with the gentle onward wave-movement of some impossible lagoon, and the moon was an amulet under the water, a sickle-shaped ornament appearing at the feet of a paddling child. Perhaps it would turn out to be a plate or some other kind of disc partially submerged in the sand, its visible part trimmed to curves by the aesthetic insistence of the sea.

High clouds are best, thought George. When they are driven higher, clouds do interesting things. Not like the ones that come close to the earth, featureless, dull, depressing, confining visibility. His whole existence had changed in the last twenty-four hours, his view of the world, his feelings about life, his energy levels. He was no longer a low cloud; he was high in the sky. Looking at this beach, this lagoon up above, he found it easy to accept the idea of a Creator, a great Artist who had designed the world so that everything would echo and reflect everything else with an irresistible sense of harmony, symmetry and metaphor.

He was shaken out of his reverie by a shouting – voices raised in anger or consternation. He walked on towards the forecourt and saw a large white van parked beside the privet trees at the back, near Rogero's car. It took him a few moments to make out the word *Ambulanza* written in reverse on the bonnet of the van. Then, coming to his senses, he remembered that this was a device aimed at eliminating a similar delay of deciphering for drivers looking in their rear mirrors. The owners of the raised voices were still hidden, but he presumed they were standing at the entrance to Rogero's apartment. He distinguished a familiar female voice, and the words

Never… Monster… Never again…

Then Mathilde appeared, flanked by two hospital orderlies in white coats. She was dishevelled, wearing dressing gown and slippers, her face bloated, perhaps from drugs, perhaps from crying. One of the hospital orderlies was carrying a suitcase. Rogero appeared behind this trio, impeccably dressed in a dark suit and carrying a travel bag.

George was now standing near enough to see that Mathilde, making her way slowly, defeatedly, towards the opened back doors of the van, had a black ceramic object, like an urn, in her hands, holding it close to her breast. He could hear quite clearly the words she spoke between the sobs, *My poor darling, my darling, my darling child…*

Rogero remained watching until the van drove out of sight. He was about to get into his own car when he noticed George standing at the corner of the house. He came over to him, and George could see a fanatical light glimmer in his eyes before the face went impassive again, businesslike.

'I'm afraid my wife is ill,' Rogero said, as if explanation had been necessary even to an evicted tenant. 'Nothing serious, it just demands hospitalization. I presume you are calling to collect your car?'

'I also wanted to say how sorry I am for the trouble I've caused you.'

'If you think apologizing is going to reinstate you, you'll have to think again.'

'And if you think sweet-talking is going to *instate* you with Barbara, you'll have to think again,' George retorted evenly.

Rogero blanched, his lip quivered, but he brazened it out. 'Don't you dare loiter around here, thinking to take liberties because I'm gone for a few days. My neighbour will be keeping an eye on the place. Goodbye and good riddance.'

'Have a nice trip.'

Piero was puzzled, more than puzzled: he was confused and disturbed. Nothing had gone right for him. Well, one venture had gone right, yielding even more than he had expected: a letter from Rome lay in front of him on his walnut desk in the living-room, one from his replacement's replacement, an old friend and colleague, conveying to him, on behalf of the board of governors, an invitation to accept the title of professor emeritus at the university, as well as reappointment to a part-time post in the faculty, in effect a sinecure. It was, he knew, as far as these cautious academics would go to apologize; but it was enough. His name would be cleared, he would accept their offer and let bygones be bygones, now that his usurper in the professorship of psychoanalysis had admitted herself to a psychiatric institution, having become a wounded healer, but in her case not because of the usual stress. Piero was now, after all, a professor of something else.

But that was the crux. Had he really become a professor of something else, or was he just a bungling dabbler? His second venture had gone disastrously wrong: George had developed bi-polar disorder, overnight it seemed, and was currently in its manic phase. There was no knowing what would happen when he sank into depression. The responsibility filled him with a sense of the tragic sublime. It had kept him awake most of the night, scarcely departed from his thoughts.

Frost etched grotesque patterns on the big windows of the living room. Winter had come back to compromise people's holiday plans. The radio had reported snow in Gubbio, on Monte Subasio, in Valfabbrica. Easter snow. Piero stood up from his desk and stamped his feet, rubbed his hands, raised them in frantic supplication to the ceiling.

'OK, OK. I win one, I lose one,' he shouted. 'But tell me what went wrong. I need to know. Please.'

He sat down at his desk again, picked up the letter from Rome, re-read it, tossed it aside. Tessa appeared at the bottom of the stairs, in her dressing gown, barefooted, hair in a tangle.

'Did you call, Papa?'

'Ah, Tessa,' he beamed. 'I never know these days if you are here or not.'

'I am staying with you for Easter, Papa. Remember?'

'Yes, yes, of course. I am very glad of that.'

'I have a message for you from Sheorge.'

Piero tensed. 'Where is he? I need to see him urgently.'

'He is gone. He left early this morning. He is driving to England.'

The professor stood up suddenly, muttering unintelligibly. He went over to where Tessa was standing, placed his hands on her shoulders. 'But why, my precious? Why? How could he leave without calling on me?'

'He was embarrassed, Papa. He was ashamed to tell you of his drinking. He broke his abstinence a few days before he went missing. He got extremely drunk. He wants me to apologize to you on his behalf.'

'Aha! So that's it.'

Tessa was surprised to see her father's look of relief. She was also glad, because she thought this might be a good time to make a confession. 'You see, Papa, I was with him last night, in his hotel.'

Piero stepped back, his eyes narrowed.

'You say you were *with him*? In what way were you with him?'

'You know, Father.'

'How could you? How could you do that, when you know what's at stake?'

'But I like Sheorge. Why shouldn't I be with him?'

'Go to your room, Tessa. Immediately.'

She began to laugh. Beetroot-faced, he raised a hand to strike her, left it suspended above her head.

'Don't you dare. I'm a big girl now, Papa.'

'You are a slut, and a married one at that!' roared Piero. 'Excuse me, please.' He walked away from her, heading for the courtyard. He wanted to go before matters got worse. He would take a long walk, cool off, try and figure it all out.

'There's another part of Sheorge's message,' Tessa called to his back, and when he didn't turn, she went after him, catching up as he fumbled at the wicket gate, the one George had been admitted through the first time he entered the house.

'The other part of the message, Papa. It's like a riddle. In English. He made me learn it by heart, and now I'm giving it to you, even though you're angry with me, in case I forget it before we speak to one another again, if we ever speak to one another again.'

He saw that she was as angry and upset as he was, and relented a little. It was a prelude to unconditional forgiveness, and she knew it.

'Well, tell me then, Daughter.'

'It goes like this: *I saw an urn at my lodging place. It may hold the ash of the child you chase.* What does it mean, Papa?'

'It means that the client has discovered what the self-appointed expert couldn't,' said Piero. He thought that maybe he should raise horses after all.

For a low-key exhibition by an unknown artist, Barbara's opening was an unqualified success. It was held at a branch public library in Hilda's borough, from four o'clock till five, in a space off the entrance hall which was normally used for various kinds of informative exhibitions to do with health and safety, environmental awareness, educational and employment opportunities, social insurance, child protection, equality issues, notification of changes in legislation and so on. It was the nearest branch of the public library to Hilda's house, and

Hilda had pestered the librarian until he had agreed to allow Barbara to instal her exhibition there for a week, between two civic displays.

The people who were gathered there for the opening almost constituted a crowd. For the most part, they were relatives and friends of Hilda, whom she had brow-beaten to put in an appearance, teacher friends of Barbara from her school, and people going to or coming from the library, lured by curiosity, coffee and finger food. The exhibition had been opened by the school's deputy headmaster, who took the opportunity to extol the enlightenment which had granted Barbara a year's leave of absence to develop her undoubted painterly talents; a fruitful break, judging from the pictures on display here, a sabbatical from which she would return to the bosom of her colleagues all the better equipped to impress upon young minds the value of art and the techniques of the brush and palette. He also mentioned that Barbara's leave of absence had been without pay, a circumstance beyond the school's control, but which warranted a deep digging by people into their pockets to support this courageous artist.

There must have been about twenty-five to thirty people there when George arrived with a bunch of flowers. He hadn't been sure if a bouquet was appropriate at an artistic opening, but had decided that his flowers were mainly by way of apology.

He was wearing his one and only suit, a grey herringbone which he had taken the trouble to press in his hotel room. But in deference to the occasion's being artistic, he had decided to mix a dash of pink shirt with the old conventional suit.

Suddenly awkward and embarrassed, he hesitated on the edge of the lively gathering, eye-searching among unfamiliar faces. Hilda spotted him, and went across to where Barbara was chatting to a tall, distinguished-looking white-haired man in a fawn smoking jacket with leather trimmings.

'Guess what the cat's just brought in?' she whispered

in Barbara's ear.

'I've seen him, Mother. Why don't you bring him over?' Barbara smiled, and went on talking to the distinguished-looking gent.

'Well, I don't know why you're here,' Hilda scolded when she had hobbled over to George. 'But apparently my daughter doesn't mind seeing you. Come on.'

George moved towards his old flame with trepidation. He picked her out from the crowd by her wine-coloured armless waistcoat and black-and-white striped jeans, and noticed with a jolt that she had cropped her hair. It was a new image and made her look younger, more boyish.

He kissed her politely on one cheek and handed her the flowers. 'You look absolutely radiant,' he said. 'Love the hair.'

'Thanks.' Barbara handed the flowers to her mother. 'Can you find something to put these in, Mum? Ask at the desk.'

Hilda went away, grumbling. Barbara looked George up and down.

'Why, George, you look much more alive than the last time I saw you.'

'It's a long story.'

'I'm sure it is, and I don't know if I want to hear it. But there's something I've been wanting to show you. Come over here.'

She brought him to a large painting, entitled 'Once and For All'. George looked at it.

'It's a pastiche of a Weeping Woman by Picasso, isn't it? Very clever, and a radical departure from your usual style.'

'Look again,' said Barbara. 'Take your time.'

George studied the picture for a while. Then he exclaimed, 'It's the bloody dog – it's Giorgio!'

'Well done!'

'It's really good, technically brilliant, very atmospheric and sombre,' he said, and she knew by his tone that he meant it.

'But why did you call it "Once and For All"?'

'Because I'll probably go back to my usual stuff after this. There was a Picasso exhibition at the Tate, including several Weeping Women from Madrid. I thought it might be good to transform a male dog, abused by his former owner, into a weeping woman. That way I felt I could understand myself and my phobia – I developed a phobia of the dogs over there, George. Of course you didn't notice, did you? Anyway, I imagined I could understand what was happening to me better by merging Giorgio and myself into an abused androgyne hybrid sort of creature. You were supposed to be in there too, but that didn't work out. I suppose you're part of the general atmosphere, the menace. It was all a bit frazzling on my nerves. I went as far as I can go there, George.'

'But I can't see how your painting will ever be the same after this.' George was still gazing appreciatively at the picture.

'It will be the same because I want it to be. Maybe it will be a little bit different. More moody, expressive. But I'm going back to landscapes and stuff. I went a bit into the dark with that one, and I don't like it – the dark, I mean.'

George was about to protest *The dark is so necessary!* but decided her opening night was not the time for their well-worn argument. He looked around the exhibition, noticed a number of red dots.

'You're doing well on the sales' side, anyway.'

'Oh, *those*. My mother has applied emotional blackmail,' said Barbara. 'It's a rent-a-crowd here. But there was some unknown, arty-looking gent who made enquiries about this picture, and the sketches leading up to it.' She gestured to a set of small pictures flanking the big one. 'He said he'd come back tomorrow.'

'Wow! Now that's something...'

'George, I don't really know what to think, seeing you here. But I've got to go and be sociable to the relatives who have shelled out. I'll be here tomorrow afternoon, if you'd like to drop by after lunch.'

'I will. I'm really sorry for my abysmal behaviour, Barbara. Maybe if I tell you what has happened to me since, you'll understand the state I was in.'

'Maybe. But I don't think it'll make any difference at this stage. Why didn't you phone earlier? Why did you leave it so long?'

'The time wasn't right. I had too much working out to do.'

'I really must go. See you tomorrow, if you like.'

'Rogero is in London, isn't he?' George asked as she turned away from him.

'Yes. He was to be here today.'

When he arrived at the library the following afternoon, George saw that Rogero was with Barbara. They were standing in the centre of the exhibition space and Barbara had a bouquet of flowers in her arm. A library attendant came along, carrying a wooden plinth. He placed it carefully some distance from another plinth on which there was a jug containing George's flowers. He went away again and came back with a vase, discreetly prised the flowers from Barbara's arm as she and Rogero continued deep in hushed conversation, and began arranging them one by one in the vase. For this library attendant, the task certainly beat cataloguing books.

George retreated towards the exit, until he thought he was reasonably inconspicuous, and watched. He noticed that Rogero's face was deathly pale and that he was gesturing weakly with his hands in a forlorn sort of way. Barbara's back looked sympathetic, and her head nodded frequently. Eventually, Rogero reached out his arms and embraced her lingeringly. Barbara put one hand tentatively on Rogero's shoulder, then the other hand, tentatively, on the other shoulder.

Seeing this, George, to his surprise, felt nothing. Immediately after feeling nothing on seeing it, he thought of Tessa and experienced the beginning of an erection. It was enormously embarrassing for him, in a private way – one part of him a total embarrassment to the other – that he should have come, libido-wise, to this pass. He felt guilty and insincere. But what was the point of pretending? He had a good mind to leave there and then; sadly, this was not out of pique or rejection, but out of shame that he didn't experience jealousy. After the months of absence, he had hoped for a return of the passion of the good old days. But while it was true that absence had made the heart grow fonder, the libido hadn't come along with the heart. All the same, he liked and admired Barbara, and wanted to make his peace. It was best to stay and face the music.

Such a look of hatred on Rogero's pallid face when, leaving hurriedly, he caught a glimpse of George skulking by the wall of the porch! But he left in a great hurry indeed, complete with valise, and George could see his former landlord hailing and running after a passing taxi before he braced himself and went up the steps to the foyer, into the exhibition space, where Barbara was chatting with the attendant.

'If a white-haired man comes looking for me,' Barbara said to the library attendant, 'tell him I'm in the café just across the road – I think it's called *Amaro*.'

She stood at the traffic lights in silence, crossed the high street briskly, entered the café a winner by several lengths from George, who discerned that her mood was not the best. They sat at a table in the brightly lit interior, waiting for two cappuccinos.

The milk-foamer hissed. A man edged past them in the

narrow space between the counter and the row of tables, his newspaper brushing against George's head. Barbara focused on a button of her pink cardigan, undid it and buttoned it again. When she raised her head, she looked pale and tired.

'I could really do without this,' she sighed. 'Why is it that even a minor achievement has to be attended by all sorts of interruptions and calamities?'

'Calamities?'

'Yes. Mathilde has just upped and died.'

'Oh my God.' George felt a tiny worm of nausea crawling in the pit of his stomach. Somewhere at the back of his mind, an expectation of this outcome had been harbouring.

The waiter brought the cappuccinos, edging them into place with a tinkle of crockery.

'Rogero is in a terrible state, as you might expect. I know Mathilde wasn't the nicest of people. She gave him an awful time. She had some hold on him, and wouldn't let go. But he wouldn't have wished death on her. I had the impression that she was under some desperate cloud.'

'The whole thing is unbelievably sad,' George said, reluctant to tell her what he had seen. 'How did she die?'

'All he knows is that she's dead – he was told by phone just this morning. He's very upset and pretty incoherent.'

George thought, He'll soon be dancing on her grave; discreetly, of course.

'And then there's Alan.' Barbara continued with her theme of interruptions and calamities. 'He's been down with the flu, and couldn't come to the exhibition, and I had to get a minder to look after him yesterday. And then there's all the relatives and friends from outside London making impossible demands, as if I should chaperone them to all the sights because they were magnanimous enough to come to the exhibition and buy some paintings.'

'You need a rest,' George said affectionately. 'I think maybe we should postpone any heart to heart until…'

'You're really not even a little bit jealous, are you, George?' Barbara accused. 'You do realise that Mathilde's death makes it easier for me to go back to Rogero's place – after a decent interval, of course.'

It flashed through George's mind that Mathilde's death might also have other implications. Would the child-ghost, reunited with its mother, be at peace? Would Mathilde find peace at last? 'I see things very differently now, Barbara,' he said. 'You've no idea what I've been through. If you did, you wouldn't expect me to – '

'I don't expect you to do anything, George. I never did expect you to do anything much.'

'Ouch!' George exclaimed light-heartedly, looking at everything kindly now in the bright refurbishment of his mind.

'I'm sorry. You're right. This is certainly not the time for a heart to heart.' She struggled with anger and tears, dismissed them. 'You have changed, though. Whatever's happened? Have you been shagging someone more to your liking?'

'What a simple explanation that would make,' George evaded. 'But something far more mysterious happened to me. Call it a descent of grace.'

'Spare me the mumbo-jumbo. I'm a good old British empiricist and always will be.'

'I wouldn't try to change you for the world.'

'More's the pity, you passive old thing.'

'After the ordeal I've gone through, I think I'll be more proactive from now on.'

'Proactive? With whom?'

'With anyone that moves above the grass.'

'I have been known to move above the grass, George.'

'Yes, I know. You're a very beautiful mover above the grass when you take the notion.'

'And there I was, thinking you were the one who didn't

take a notion. Seriously though, I have to think of Alan. Things are different when there's a child. And you – you're really not interested in children, are you? I need a good father for Alan, and you're not it.'

'And you think he is?'

'It's late in the day, and he's the best of two. He really likes Alan. And he's crazy about me. That's a big plus at my age… But here comes my latest white knight. Oh no, he's got more flowers!'

A white-haired man in a suede overcoat came in the door of the café, carrying a large bouquet, offered it to Barbara with a fluttering of petals.

'I hope this is not an inopportune time. Congratulations on a fascinating exhibition. As I believe I told you yesterday, I'm very interested in buying some of your pictures.' He turned to George. 'Do you mind awfully?'

George rose. 'Not at all. I was going anyway. See you, Barbara.' He kissed her.

'When?'

'Soon. I'll phone.'

'We haven't finished catching up.'

'Of course we haven't. Only beginning. Good luck with the exhibition.'

George paused at the door, listening to the loud, pompous voice of the white-haired buyer, possibly another suitor, watching Barbara's response. Look at her, he thought, so confident, such poise despite all the pressures, talking to that toff and not in the least bit cheesy or sycophantic. A natural, at her ease in a world of artifice. (Was that a slight twitch he felt in his groin, the faint stirring of a new growth?)

He had a lot to ruminate on, walking back along the high street to the underground. A few shops were closing, putting up their shutters. People walked along with him and came against him, but George was oblivious, euphoric, in a different space.

He was thinking, It's true that there is much to be confronted and dealt with, but my problems are now of nature and life, they are not unnatural, intangible, supernatural and deathly. I will tackle them with tenderness and zest. I will say Yes to life, at last.

'And how is my little treasure today then?'

He heard it clearly, and froze. It was his uncle's voice.

Someone coming along behind bumped his shoulder, muttered disparagingly and passed. He heard a child screaming. Gasping for breath, he was sure he was going to die from fear. But his eyes were wildly alert, scanning the surroundings.

Just a few yards ahead of him, there was a hatted figure in a long dark overcoat. A little girl, about four or five, a school satchel on her back, came running from a gateway on to the pavement, shouting 'Daddy! Daddy!' and jumped into the man's arms, threw her arms around his neck as he lifted her; splayed her legs around his waist. The man walked back past George, carrying his little treasure, her gold-ringleted head resting on his shoulder.

George moved away from the centre of the pavement, leaned against the railings, and stayed there for a long time, wheezing his way through aftershocks of fear and revulsion. Other children were coming out of the playschool, parents arriving to greet them and bring them away. But he did not hear his uncle's phrase again; these mothers and fathers used different endearments – 'darling' or 'sweetheart' – or simply called their children by name. There were no more little treasures to be collected.

Gradually, his terror subsided, gave way to relief; his breathing became more regular. He had to admit that the professor was right: it had taken this incident to force the recognition that he was damaged and only at the beginning of repair. He found it hard to be reconciled with the diagnosis of someone as loopy as Piero, a wounded healer if ever there was one.

Then he realized that simply by standing where he was, watching the children as they came out, not meeting any one of them, he himself could arouse suspicion as a possible pervert. All the more so because his breathing was still heavy. It was a consideration that gave him the will to resume his walk to the underground.

On the tube, although still shaken by what he had witnessed, he began to have mixed feelings about it. He felt a sudden pang of jealousy for the little ringleted girl: hers was a very different way of being treasured than his had been – one that didn't steal childhood, but gave it.

It may have been true, but it wasn't very nice of Barbara to say that he didn't have any interest in children. And Barbara had made other catty remarks, like saying she had never expected him to do anything much. But maybe it wasn't too late for him to overcome his past and bring up a child in a blessedly normal way. And how would Barbara know what he was capable of now, after what he had gone through? He found himself indulging a catty little fantasy in which he re-introduced her to Tessa: *Barbara, this is Tessa. You remember her, don't you, from Rogero's soirée?* He would have to be much franker and more assertive with her when they met to continue their catching up.

There was a background noise in George's hotel bedroom. He became aware of it as he sat at the dressing table in his pyjamas, sipping a glass of wine and writing a heading on hotel stationery for a list he intended to compile: *Immediate Priorities.*

The noise was familiar to him from spending nights in

hotels, in other people's homes and in apartments he had rented over the years. It could have been coming from the heating system's boiler or some other everyday appliance. It was a strong, pulsating sound, with slight changes of register from which it constantly returned to its dominant mode, and George didn't think it intrusive like the screech of a house alarm, coming close and going distant, or the unpredictable growling of traffic. Instead, he found it comforting and didn't want to know its origin because he preferred to imagine it was the throbbing of life's continuance – some vast, genial, unsophisticated machine that underwrote the conditions of existence, that guaranteed the passage of life from one generation to the next, and had an army of maintenance angels standing by to fix malfunctions, to keep it going at all costs. It was the sound made by Being itself as it moved through time. And he felt as he listened that it was bringing him back to himself after the whirligig he had just been through, and he was grateful and decided there was no immediate need to compile his list of immediate priorities. He climbed into bed and allowed the machine of existence to lull him asleep.

ACKNOWLEDGEMENTS

Thanks to my wife, Margaret Farrelly, and my literary agent Jonathan Williams, for reading early drafts of this novel and for their helpful comments and their assistance in other ways. Likewise to John Davies, Meredith Collins, Sarah Fretwell-Jex and Tom Slingsby for constructive criticism and encouragement from their reading of later versions.

Thanks also to novelist and playwright John MacKenna for his generosity in reading the novel at short notice before printing.

And to Fernando Trilli and the late Paul Cahill for welcoming me, with Margaret and my son Conor, to their farmhouse in Umbria and making our stay in Italy a golden dream rather than 'a year's midnight'. And to those others who befriended us into the culture, Gianni and Andreina, Piero and Simonetta, Giuliana and Leonardo and their families, Eiléan and Macdara, Rita, and the teachers and children of Scuola Materna Villa-Soccorso which my son attended. And many others.

THE AUTHOR

Ciaran O'Driscoll is one of the leading authors of his generation. He has won the James Joyce Literary Millennium Prize, the Patrick and Katherine Kavanagh Fellowship in Poetry and he was elected to Aosdána in 2007. Born in Callan, Co. Kilkenny in 1943, he now lives in Limerick.